BRYONY ROSEHURST

First Comes Marriage

Copyright © 2023 by Bryony Rosehurst

All rights reserved. No part of this publication may be reproduced, stored or transmitted in any form or by any means, electronic, mechanical, photocopying, recording, scanning, or otherwise without written permission from the publisher. It is illegal to copy this book, post it to a website, or distribute it by any other means without permission.

This novel is entirely a work of fiction. The names, characters and incidents portrayed in it are the work of the author's imagination. Any resemblance to actual persons, living or dead, events or localities is entirely coincidental.

Bryony Rosehurst asserts the moral right to be identified as the author of this work.

First edition

This book was professionally typeset on Reedsy.
Find out more at reedsy.com

Content Warnings

- Strong language
- Mentions of past infidelities
- Mentions of alcohol and drugs

Chapter One

"You summoned me?" Charlie Dean kicked her legs up on the desk, crossing them at the ankles, and peering at her manager over the shaded lenses of her Ray-Bans. Jed cast her a scathing look. His face was slightly redder than usual, his shirtsleeves rolled to his elbows as he marched into the office and sat down across from her. Charlie almost smirked. It took a lot to rattle one of the industry's finest.

"I could strangle you," he said, crossing his arms over his chest and piercing her with his dark, disapproving gaze.

A tremor danced through her but she paid it no heed, turning her lips into a bright grin instead. "That's kinky even for you, Jed. And at," she checked the time on her phone, "eleven o'clock in the morning? At least buy me brunch first."

"Do you think this is funny?" His stubbled jaw set squarely, he leaned as though he was the stern teacher and she was his erring student. It was strange, being treated like a child at twenty-eight. Apparently, when one became a famous musician, one also lost any right to independence or dignity. Then again, Charlie might

First Comes Marriage

have thrown some of that away herself over the years.

Especially last night.

She pulled her boots off the desk and began playing with a ball of elastic bands instead, trying to hide the trembling in her fingers as she *snap, snap, snapped*. "I think it's not *not* funny."

"You went on stage drunk." He slapped *OK! Magazine* down in front of her. Her face was plastered on the glossy cover along with a pixelated, grainy photograph of her slamming her guitar on the stage and leaving it in splinters. The caption, *A bit too rock 'n' roll, Charlie Dean?* was printed beneath.

"You had a fucking meltdown." Another magazine. This one *Hello.* Charlie hadn't made the main image in favour of a celebrity pregnancy announcement, but she'd still managed to earn the right corner. "You hit one of your fans with a piece of your bloody guitar!"

"Not on purpose," she replied dryly, tearing her eyes away from the magazine before she thought too much about it. "I signed it for them afterwards. They were actually quite happy about it. It'll sell for thousands on eBay."

It hadn't been her finest hour, she could admit. And fine, she'd been a little bit drunk and a little bit angry after finding out her ex-bandmates had decided to re-form without her to release a new single. As though she hadn't been their frontwoman. As though she hadn't been the face of Ghost Song since the age of eighteen.

Her grip on the elastic band ball tightened.

"They're saying you've gone off the rails," Jed said, fiddling with his thick thumb ring and leaning back in his chair. "Again."

She rolled her eyes. "All rock stars go off the rails. Thought you liked my bad girl rep."

"I liked your charisma. Your edge. But this…" His lips pursed

Chapter One

thinly, and he shook his head. "This is a kid throwing a tantrum, Charlie. This is how some of the most talented people in the industry end up becoming washed-up nobodies. Or worse. People don't pay to watch you make a fucking mess of yourself. After last year, I thought you'd understand that."

She scowled at the mention of last year's incident, pushing her sunglasses onto her head to make sure he saw. It was forbidden territory. Besides, she wasn't sure what they expected. They'd been pushing this solo tour for months. Hundreds of gigs, a different city every night, recording her second album as soon as she got back to the tour bus. It was only normal that she'd needed to blow off steam. To remind them that they couldn't control her, that she was a person and not a performing monkey. She hadn't intended to go quite so far with it, but that was the drink's fault. She made stupid decisions under the influence, just like everyone else. And she wasn't usually prone to getting drunk before a concert, but... it had been a hard day. She would have been flat, depressing, if she'd gone out there with her mood so low, and that would be even worse. At least this was something to talk about. At least this kept her unpredictable, exciting.

"You've turned really boring in your old age," she quipped. Jed huffed. He was only in his mid-thirties, but she liked to tease. Usually, he'd give her something back. They'd keep up the banter. Friends rather than co-workers. But he wasn't playing today, and that left her feeling cold.

"Am I getting through to you at all?"

She pretended to think for a moment. "No."

"Right. Of course not." He stood up, leaning over the desk so she could no longer avoid looking at him. "Do you want to keep your career? Because last night seemed an awful lot like

3

First Comes Marriage

you didn't."

She only shrugged, biting her tongue. Being a musician was all she'd ever wanted, but it didn't feel like enough anymore. She'd been... lonely— *shudder* —since going solo. Having a tour bus to herself wasn't quite the same as sharing it with four other people. Making music on her own with nobody to bounce off....

She'd started all of this with her friends because she'd liked being in a band. Liked being part of something. But now she was part of nothing, and the stage was too big without them. They were moving on without her. They didn't need her anymore. Didn't want her.

She absently scratched her nails against the Ghost Song logo tattooed on the inside of her arm.

Jed raised his brows as though he'd been expecting a slightly different response. "Well?"

But what would she do if she quit? There was nothing else. She wasn't good at anything but playing and writing music. Where would she go without it? Not home. She barely kept in touch with her family, and she had no friends but the ones she worked with.

"You know I do," she said finally, as much as it pained her to be open about it.

"Then get your arse in gear and stop fucking up." He straightened, sighing. "I was just on the phone with Jazz." Her publicist. She supposed that meant more lectures were still to come. "She's doing some serious damage control, but... we have an idea of how to get people to like you again."

"Oh, goodie," Charlie deadpanned, voice dripping with sarcasm. "Let me guess. Visit a children's hospital. Play with puppies. Donate to charity."

"Nope." He lowered back into his seat and swivelled from

Chapter One

side to side like some sort of evil villain in a James Bond movie. "Try reality TV."

A scoff fell from her, almost causing her to choke on her chewing gum, which she'd used in an attempt to hide her terrible hangover breath. "Fuck off."

"It's a good opportunity," Jed shrugged. "They've been trying to get you on this one for years. I always turned them down to maintain your little," he sprinkled his fingers in her general direction, "'girl misunderstood' persona. But I think we passed the station for 'misunderstood' a few stops ago and are quickly delving into 'spoilt, disgraceful brat' territory. And nobody likes those. Nobody buys their albums."

"Please, don't water it down on my account," she muttered to hide her sting. She never used to care what people thought about her, but that was another symptom of her solo career. She was carrying her own name now, and only she and her publicist could decide how she came across. She didn't particularly care where she ranked in the charts, but... the thought of losing her career suddenly felt real. What would she do then? Go back to Manchester, a washed-up nobody just like Jed had said with no friends, no career, no passion.

Fuck.

"You know," she continued, "if I were a man, I'd just be really fuckin' cool. But because I'm a woman, I'm a 'spoilt brat.'"

He rolled his eyes. "Maybe so. But man or woman, I'd refuse to keep managing someone I can't trust to do their job properly. Are you going to let me tell you about this gig or not?"

"I'm not eating kangaroo balls on TV. I don't care if I never work again." *I'm A Celebrity... Get Me Out of Here!* might have been fun to watch, but all the money in the world wouldn't make Charlie want to jet off to Australia to camp in a jungle for

First Comes Marriage

two weeks.

He snorted, "No kangaroo balls involved in this one."

"And I'm not going to live in a house with a bunch of weirdos who argue over cereal."

Jed tilted his head. "You're getting closer, but no. Wasn't *Big Brother* cancelled years ago?"

"Alright then," Charlie said slowly as she clasped her hands over her unsettled stomach impatiently, "enlighten me."

He scratched his jaw as though trying to draw the moment out. Finally, he asked, "What's your stance on arranged marriages?"

Charlie broke into a peal of laughter. Only when she noticed that Jed hadn't joined in did she realise that he was serious.

Chapter Two

Tamara Hewitt had never imagined her second wedding to involve quite so many cameras and producers. She kept that newly whitened beam on her face as her makeup artist and hair stylist fussed around her, fiddling nervously with her bracelet.

"Remind me why I agreed to this again?" she asked, sparing a sidelong glance for her agent and best friend Nadine, who seemed quite happy sipping the hotel's complimentary champagne while one of Tamara's stylists did her nails. Her chestnut hair was in rollers and a gown covered her dusty pink bridesmaid's dress to avoid any disasters.

"To find love," Nadine replied with a wistful sigh. "And to," she cleared her throat, glancing at the cameras before whispering, "dispel any of those nasty rumours left over from your divorce."

Of course. Why had Tamara bothered to ask? She had to admit, though, it was nice to get a second chance after the catastrophe of her short, not-so-sweet marriage to well-known actor Dominic Lowell. It wasn't as though she was naive enough

First Comes Marriage

to believe celebrities forced together on her favourite reality TV show, *First Comes Marriage*, could actually fall in love, but... she'd exhausted all other options. Nobody would touch her with a ten-foot barge pole after Dominic had dragged her name through the mud, accusing her of cheating. Which wasn't true. He was paranoid and controlling. Projecting his own guilt, perhaps, because it was he who had been cheating, and he hadn't wanted anyone to find out that was the reason for their speedy divorce. She just needed somebody to restore her faith in the dating game. She needed a second chance at love.

And she supposed marrying a stranger was as good a way to get it as any, even if she'd been coaxed into it for the sake of her waning popularity.

She chewed her bottom lip, which led to a scowl from her makeup artist who had just applied a fine coat of gloss over a subtle matte pink lipstick.

"Are you nervous, Tamara?" one of the producers asked, and she felt the heat of the camera zooming in on her face.

She stared at her reflection, taking a deep breath. "Just a little bit."

"What type of person do you hope you'll be matched with?"

She fidgeted, glad when her makeup artist ordered her to close her eyes. She still saw the bright white vanity lights stamped behind her lids while glittery eye shadow was dusted and mascara smeared. "I'm not sure. I don't think I've ever really known what I want, and that's why I struggle so much to find the right person. Maybe I should hope for the opposite of what I usually go for." She laughed. "Maybe that'll make it more successful than my past relationships. I clearly don't choose the best people. It would be nice to be matched with someone kind. Understanding. Patient." Not somebody who tore her down

Chapter Two

over and over the way Dominic had.

"Do you have any deal breakers?"

She batted her lids and looked to Nadine for support. If she said "cheating," the nation would label her the world's worst hypocrite. Nadine gave her a nod of support though. *You got this. Just be open.* It had been her mantra all week, but it was difficult to be open with half-a-dozen cameras pointed at her, even if she was used to prancing about in her lingerie for photoshoots. Revealing her plus-size body, putting it on display for everyone to judge, had been one thing, but this... after the blows she'd already faced to her self-esteem from the divorce....

"I think I just need somebody who's understanding. I'm a patient person, but if they lack empathy or sensitivity, I'll find it difficult to be with them." She smiled. *There.* It wasn't a lie, and she didn't have to tread Dominic territory to get there. Now she just had to put up with another six to twelve weeks of calculating answers to every question while the whole country watched her marry a stranger.

"What are you hoping to get out of this?" the producer continued.

Tamara swallowed, her heart leaping into her throat when the stylists stepped back.

She brushed through her blonde curls and blotted her lips, sitting forward in her chair. "Love," she said, perhaps more sincerely than any of the other answers she'd given yet. Her voice wobbled. "I hope to find love."

* * *

Charlie considered making a run for it. She could pull a *Runaway Bride.* In a white, tailored jumpsuit and brogues, she

First Comes Marriage

wouldn't have to worry about tripping over her dress's trail or twisting an ankle on high heels. She was set for it, really, as though her stylist had known. The corsetted top half might pose a problem for her lungs, but she only had to make it off the Spanish beach, past the cameras.

As though sensing her desire to dash, Jed hovered behind her, his warmth prickling the back of her tattooed neck. "It's only twelve weeks at most," he reminded quietly, maintaining a warm smile for the guests watching from their benches. Some of them were hired extras, others friends and family. Not Charlie's, mind. She hadn't invited hers. Hadn't even told them. The only person she had here was Jed and her drummer, Angelica, who sat on the front row to flash Charlie the occasional thumbs-up.

"I'll marry you off to a complete stranger and see how twelve weeks feels to you," she muttered, glad when a stiff breeze whispered off the sea. The waves crashed behind them. A bloody beach wedding, as though things couldn't get any worse. Not only did she have to live with cameras in front of her face while she pretended to be happily married to a stranger for twelve weeks, but she also had sand in her socks and her eyes, the sun beating down so she had to squint. Most people's idea of a romantic fantasy was her idea of hell.

She didn't even want to think about who might walk down the aisle in—she checked her phone, stowed away in a hidden pocket—ten minutes. She hadn't dared to imagine. She could only hope it wouldn't be one of those "influencers" who usually appeared on this type of shitty reality TV for their five minutes of fame. She couldn't handle that.

"Put your phone away." Jed gritted his teeth, giving her a scolding poke. "You're at your own bloody wedding. Give it here."

Chapter Two

"It's not a *real* wedding." She puffed out a breath but still surrendered her phone when he held out his hand. He confiscated it, tucking it into the inside pocket of his linen suit.

"It's a real marriage."

Sandra, the woman who had interviewed Charlie when she'd signed up, appeared beneath the rose-covered wedding arch then, shooting an optimistic smile Charlie's way. She was named one of the "Cupids" of the show, but her real job was, apparently, "relationship expert". *Definitely not a thing*, Charlie thought. She'd just slapped the word "expert" there to make it sound like one. It was like Charlie calling herself a potato expert because she liked chips.

"Good to see you again, Charlie. Are you excited?" Sandra smoothed down her pink, bodycon dress and neatened a stack of notes, her script. Her teeth were pearly white in the sun.

"Hmm."

Sandra's eyes shone just as brightly. "I think you'll be very happy with your match today."

Charlie raised an unconvinced eyebrow. "I'm sure."

"Don't worry. Plenty of people get jitters on the big day."

Charlie almost wanted to laugh. The churning in her stomach was not nearly as light and fluttery as jitters. She felt... trapped. Pissed off. Already done. But Jed had been right about the publicity, as much as it pained her to say it. She was very much hated by fans who'd once adored her. Her album sales had plummeted dramatically since her little... outburst. People claimed she was "cancelled" and "irrelevant" and her music had been "shitty to begin with." Her record label had threatened to terminate her contract. Meanwhile, Ghost Song was thriving with their newest release, though the single merely mimicked Charlie's old lyrics and melodies. People didn't see that though.

First Comes Marriage

They only saw a woman who had made a mistake and deserved to be wiped from the industry because of it. Still, she'd come back from worse.

"How are you feeling, Charlie?" A camera was shoved in her face, one of the show's producers behind it.

Jed's finger dug into her shoulder blade, and she forced a grim smile. "Oh, wonderful."

"Nervous?"

She wiped her sweaty palms on her chiffon bottoms. "Hmmmm. Yep."

The producer shifted, apparently discontent with the lacklustre responses. "Who are you hoping to see walk down the aisle?"

"A woman, I hope," she deadpanned.

Sandra let out a high-pitched laugh. "I'm sure your bride will love that sense of humour."

Charlie wasn't joking, though. She'd seen shows where people were married off to robots. Dating shows where people wore masks to resemble pandas among other zoo animals. Reality TV producers would do anything for a bit of shock value. No amount of money would drive her to that though, and she started bouncing on her heels just to make sure her legs were warmed up should she decide to go back to her exit strategy.

The camera people filtered away from Charlie. Some of them lined the sandy aisle while others loitered close by, ready to get Charlie's reaction. She vowed not to give them even a hint of what simmered beneath her calm exterior.

The violinist began to play a soft, keening instrumental cover of "Will You Still Love Me Tomorrow?" and Charlie had to fight the urge not to cringe. She was instructed to keep her back to the aisle until she was given the cue, and she closed her eyes

Chapter Two

as a wave of dread washed over her. Was her career honestly worth this?

Maybe if it wasn't all she had, it wouldn't be. Maybe she'd driven herself to this by being so careless, so detached from anything but her music.

Jed squeezed her wrist before taking a seat beside Angelica, and then she was on her own. She was absolutely certain she was going to throw up.

"Ready?" Sandra asked.

"Nope." *Not even a little bit.* She tried to convince herself that it didn't matter. There was no use worrying about a stupid publicity stunt. But she would have to spend every day with the person at the end of the aisle for twelve weeks — or at least until they were voted out by the public after the first six weeks. There would be no escape, no going to the studio to blow off steam or getting drunk at an afterparty. They'd be confined to Valentine's Village, an estate of cottages and holiday homes in the middle of Nowhere, England. The prize for the couple who won would go to their chosen charity, but Charlie doubted she'd get that far.

She could leave, she decided. Whenever she was ready, as soon as she'd done her part and cleaned up her image, she could make up some fake reason to exit the show. She wouldn't have to stay forever. Just long enough to get people to like her again.

She took a deep breath and straightened, steeling herself as the song reached the chorus. And then Sandra gave the signal for her to turn around, and Charlie did.

She immediately wished she hadn't.

The bride walking down the aisle was familiar — not this version of her, but a glossier one in magazines and posters. Charlie couldn't remember her name, only that she was abso-

First Comes Marriage

lutely certain the woman was a model. She wore everything Charlie refused to wear: a glamorous, fitted, off-the-shoulder dress made of lace and sparkly tulle that moulded to her wide and unpredictable curves. The train spanned half of the aisle as she neared, picking up sand, and her veil almost swallowed the guests whole when the wind blew.

Charlie grimaced. She was so… traditional. A complete poster bride, elegant and beautiful, but not much beyond the tulle. Blonde hair cascaded around her round face, makeup powdered to glossy, nude perfection. Not Charlie's type at all. Not even a little bit.

She offered Charlie a watery smile as she finally approached, clutching a bouquet of pink and white roses that matched the arch. Charlie couldn't find it in her to return it, instead looking her up and down and wondering how on earth they were going to pretend to be happily married. It was so clear that they were polar opposites. If Charlie was whiskey, the bride was champagne. Charlie couldn't spot one tattoo, and she'd never spent longer than fifteen minutes doing her makeup in her life. She didn't do Instagram. Didn't do models at all. If they were at a party together, Charlie would wonder what the bride was doing there and then spend the rest of the night well away. She probably listened to Ed Sheeran: a harrowing thought.

"Hello," the bride said quietly. Something sparkled in her eyes: knowing, perhaps? Maybe she recognised Charlie. It would be difficult not to after the last few weeks. "I'm Tamara."

God, even her name was objectionably pretty. Charlie replied flatly, "Charlie." She shifted on her feet awkwardly.

"It's nice to… marry you." She laughed at her own joke, and Charlie wanted to cringe even harder.

"Yeah."

Chapter Two

One bridesmaid from the long line of women wearing ghastly pink took Tamara's bouquet, leaving Tamara to gaze uncertainly at Charlie. Alright, she was ridiculously gorgeous in a classic sort of way, even more so now, with her pale blue eyes lightened by the sun, but... she was just... not Charlie's cup of tea. Not someone she could see herself liking, even as a friend.

"This is so weird," Tamara gulped, shaking her hands out nervously. "Sorry. I'm nervous. You look really nice, by the way."

"Cheers," Charlie replied. "Nice, er, dress."

"You're northern?"

She nodded. Tamara very clearly wasn't, with a posh London accent that made her sound royal.

"Shall we get started?" Sandra asked. Everyone sat, the weight of their gazes drowning Charlie. She faced the front, no longer able to look at anyone, including her bride. God, this was a colossal mistake.

"This marriage starts off unconventional," said Sandra without so much as glancing at her cue cards, "but we hope that Tamara and Charlie find something real and beautiful on this beach today. As relationship experts, we based this match on both their similarities and their differences, qualities that will complement and challenge one another. Charlie, Tamara," she motioned to each of them in turn, "the Cupids wish you the best of luck as you begin this journey together. Shall we begin the vows?"

Tamara's bridesmaid handed her a piece of notepaper, and Charlie's stomach twinged. *Fuck.* She hadn't written her bloody vows. She'd pushed it all aside in the hopes none of it was real.

"I'll start, I suppose," Tamara said shakily. Her eyes locked on Charlie's, framed by dark lashes. "Charlie. I know this isn't

First Comes Marriage

the usual way of getting married, but the usual way never quite worked for me. I want you to know that, today, I'm choosing to wear my heart on my sleeve once again in the hopes that this time, it *will* work."

Oh, bloody hell. Charlie prayed this was all for the cameras and Tamara didn't actually expect this to be a real marriage. She pressed her lips into a thin line, wondering if that glint in Tamara's eyes was a sign of real, raw hope.

"I promise that I'll always try," Tamara continued. "I promise that, on the days where you can only give twenty percent, I'll be the other eighty. I promise that I'll laugh at your jokes and watch your favourite films. I promise that I'll sing too often and probably annoy you sometimes, too. But mostly, I promise that I'm ready to be a strong, reliable, loving partner, one that you'll be proud to have by your side. I'm excited to get to know you and grateful that I now get to call you my wife."

Charlie used the sun as an excuse to shield her face, swallowing down her nausea slowly. A few of the bridesmaids were in tears. She looked at Jed as though to say, *I didn't sign up for this*, but he only tipped his head in encouragement, his jaw clenched stiffly.

"Charlie?" Sandra asked after a few moments of silence.

"Er... Okay. I'm..." She sucked in a breath, trying to conjure the right words that would make her seem as though she wasn't completely winging it. But for some reason, all that kept coming back was one of her old songs. *Fuck it.* Lyrics were as good as vows, anyway. "Tamara, I'm good at being alone, but I hope maybe..." She felt like an idiot. A first-class idiot. "I hope maybe you and I can build a home. Together." She scratched the back of her neck, looking away when a tear sprang to Tamara's eye. Surely she wasn't buying this.

Chapter Two

Maybe she was an actress rather than a model. Maybe Charlie had confused her for someone else.

Sandra, the cameras, Jed, all watched her steadily as she stuttered and stumbled. It was as though they were screaming at her to try harder. Do better.

"I suppose I can promise you that this marriage will always be an unpredictable adventure. You know, I'm probably not what you expected or hoped, but I'll always surprise you. I'll never take anything too seriously. I'm with you in this and I'm looking forward to the future." The future where Charlie could get out of this and move on with her life. The future where thousands of people weren't watching her on TV. The future where things went back to normal again.

Tamara smiled, but a shadow darkened her face that hadn't been there a minute ago.

"Good. Without further ado..." A producer handed the rings to Sandra, and Charlie took the larger silver band from Sandra's palm. Tamara followed. "Tamara, do you take Charlie as your wife?"

"I do." She said it quietly as though she wasn't sure. Good. Better she knew now that Charlie wasn't in this for a relationship. Charlie extended her left hand, and Tamara slid the ring onto her fourth finger carefully, her manicured nails grazing Charlie's skin. The wedding band covered an old miniature rose tattoo below her knuckle.

"Charlie, do you take Tamara as your wife?"

"Yep." Charlie didn't waste much time slipping on Tamara's ring, still refusing to meet her piercing gaze as she did.

"I now pronounce you wife and wife. Congratulations!"

Everybody clapped and cheered, and Tamara's fingers slotted between hers to face their audience, cameras included. Charlie forced a smile, but she'd never been more uncomfortable and less herself in her life. The show might have been an act, but the marriage was real. She'd signed the certificate last week. She wore a ring on her finger. She was supposed to be somebody's *wife*.

"Are you happy?" Tamara asked, flashing a bright set of straight teeth. Dimples bracketed her beam.

Charlie only pursed her lips. "I will be after a drink," she admitted, and could only hope that the microphone strapped under her clothes wouldn't pick it up.

Chapter Three

Charlie Dean was the last person in the world Tamara would have expected to marry today. She'd recognised the chiselled, short-haired musician instantly, as anybody else would, and her stomach had plummeted.

But she'd tried her best to put any preconceived ideas influenced by the press aside. She knew too well how the tabloids manipulated and lied about people, and just because she'd seen a few negative articles about Charlie recently, that didn't mean they were true.

Only, Charlie wasn't exactly the warmest bride to marry. She'd barely looked at Tamara through the whole ceremony, and after talking to the producers about their initial impressions, they now stood stiffly hand-in-hand while a photographer hopped around them, ordering to position one leg here and look that way and smile a little bit more. Tamara was used to it, but Charlie kept sighing as though she'd rather be anywhere else.

"So," Tamara said between shots, rearranging her train

First Comes Marriage

awkwardly on the sand. The wedding party were already enjoying cocktail hour in the restaurant on the pier, something she envied greatly at the moment. "Tell me about you. Why this show?"

Charlie only shrugged, her dark hair barely ruffling in the balmy sea breeze. "Why not?" was her only reply. Tamara had a feeling that if the cameras weren't on, the answer might have been different.

She looked away, ignoring the pricking in her eyes and the heat in her cheeks. She'd expected somebody who'd at least feign interest in her, but Charlie was cold as ice. Unreachable. That hope in her chest shattered like ceramic. Though attractive in a grungy, effortless sort of way, Charlie wasn't exactly her type, and she'd known that as soon as she'd seen her, but... Tamara at least deserved a bit of attention, didn't she?

Scratch that. She deserved to find somebody who would *worship* her.

"Charlie, can you look this way and put your hand on Tamara's hip?"

Charlie stiffened as she sidled closer to Tamara, her hand barely hovering on her round, jutting waist. "Sorry," she muttered in Tamara's ear.

Tamara faked a smile. "Why? You're my wife now. You're welcome to touch me." And then her cheeks burned as she realised what she'd said. The double meaning that could be tugged from her words. "I mean, don't feel uncomfortable."

"But I do. This is fucking weird," Charlie muttered.

They'd sailed past "weird" hours ago, but Tamara was trying her best. She really was. "It doesn't have to be. We can just take things slow. Get to know one another. I'd love to hear about your music."

20

Chapter Three

"How about you tilt your head up for a kiss, Tamara?" the photographer bellowed.

Tamara cringed. Maybe taking things slow wasn't an option. She held her breath as she leaned into Charlie's tall frame, her back to Charlie's front. She was slim, sinewy almost, but she towered over Tamara all the same and felt sturdy enough. So Tamara curled her hand around the nape of Charlie's neck and tipped her chin to the sky, convincing herself this was just a normal photoshoot. The ones she did every day.

Charlie leaned down but froze well before Tamara could kiss her, their cheeks grazing instead. Tamara looked up at her, meeting her dark, eyeliner-ringed eyes in question. Charlie was more interested in her shoulder, even as her free hand rested on the other side of Tamara's waist. The sun's rays slanted between them, leaving her irises amber.

"I don't bite," Tamara whispered.

"Well, that's a shame." The corner of Charlie's mouth twitched as the photographer continued to snap away, crouching and getting them from all angles. Tamara's face blazed, unsure if that was humour or something else, something more flirtatious.

Until the hollow, flat expression Charlie had sported all through the wedding returned.

Tamara tried to pull her back. "What's your stance on Hawaiian pizza?"

Charlie frowned. "Pardon?"

"Pineapple on pizza. Yay or nay?"

"I... don't really care," Charlie spoke slowly, as though Tamara was too slow to keep up.

"Turn to face each other and hold hands again?" the photographer asked.

Tamara pulled away from Charlie's touch, lacing their fingers

First Comes Marriage

together. Their wedding rings glinted in the afternoon sun, and her stomach twisted. Marrying a stranger had never sounded like the best idea, but this... it was like drawing blood from a stone, trying to get anything from her new wife.

"A little to the right so the sun's between you?"

She stepped back, and Charlie followed.

"I don't think fruit should be on pizza." Tamara had no idea why she was still talking. "I'm meat feast all the way."

"People are dying and the planet is burning, but okay."

Though emotionless, the words stung. So that's what it was. Charlie thought that Tamara was superficial, only caring about things that didn't matter. Maybe she knew she was a model. She wouldn't be the first to assume from her occupation and appearance that Tamara was an airhead.

Her hands went limp in Charlie's. "I'm just trying to get to know you. I don't see what global catastrophes have to do with that."

Charlie's glance fell to the cameras trained on them. She licked her lips, a muscle feathering in her jaw. "Let's just get the bloody photographs out of the way."

Heart sinking, Tamara could only agree, following the photographer's orders without a word. Even after all this time, being disliked felt like a punch to the gut, and she hated the insecure part of her that always needed validation.

She clearly wasn't going to get it from Charlie Dean. She might as well get used to the cold shoulder.

* * *

Charlie gulped down her second glass of Jack and Coke. The waiters had offered around champagne when everyone had

Chapter Three

seated themselves for the outdoor meal beneath a large gazebo, but she needed something stronger. She almost wanted to ask for a couple of shots just to take the edge off.

The food was shit. The majority of the plate was empty, with only a dollop of chicken and puréed God-knows-what in the centre. Tamara spent most of her time talking to her bridesmaid and fluffing her hair, and Charlie used the opportunity to throw plenty of glares Jed's way.

Finally, after a dessert of poached pear that Charlie didn't touch, he shuffled down the table to talk to her, the cameras following him all the while. "So," he leaned on his elbows, glancing past Charlie to get Tamara's attention too, "how does it feel to be a newlywed?"

"I'll answer that when I'm a little bit drunker."

Jed rolled his eyes and shook Tamara's hand across Charlie's drink. "I'm Jed, Charlie's manager. It's a pleasure to meet you. You're a model, aren't you?"

"Yep." Tamara's smile was polite, friendly, even. She seemed to have given up small talk with Charlie after the photos, but she was still trying with everyone else. For the cameras or the sake of the guests, Charlie didn't know.

"That's certainly different to what Charlie is used to."

"Oh, I bet it is." She shot Charlie a pointed, sidelong look as she plucked the strawberry from her champagne and took a bite.

"I think I know your ex-husband, actually. Dominic. Our paths cross from time to time." Jed raked his fingers through his red, trimmed beard.

Charlie couldn't help but watch Tamara carefully. She shifted in her seat, her throat bobbing, and she reached for a napkin, folding it over and over with fidgeting fingers. "Hmm. Of

First Comes Marriage

course. Yeah. I'm sure he has some... interesting stories to tell about me."

"Dominic who?" Charlie asked, raising an eyebrow.

"Lowell," Jed said. "The actor."

For the first time that day, Charlie failed at hiding her surprise. She'd heard of Dominic Lowell. Most people had. He'd been in some of the biggest shows and movies in the UK — and the world, predictably, had grown obsessed with him.

"So you've been married before," she said dryly. "I can't imagine why you'd want to put yourself through it a second time. Especially like this."

Jed kicked Charlie's shin under the table. "Honestly, between you and me," he leaned in close, covering the microphone pinned to his collar with his hand, "he's a bit of an arsehole. Can't stand the guy."

A laugh bubbled from Tamara at that, and she seemed to melt with relief. "On that, we can agree."

"Would you two like to get married instead?" Charlie questioned, glancing between them. "You can gossip about celebrities all you want, then."

Tamara sat back, her jaw set and her chin wobbling. Not for the first time that night, either. Charlie was beginning to worry that she truly had come on the show for... well, a marriage. A real one. It annoyed her, somehow. Real people didn't get married on TV. Real people weren't this desperate to be liked. If Tamara wanted a real relationship, this was the last place to find it, and Charlie shouldn't have had to feel guilty about being realistic.

"Charlie," Jed said firmly. "Can I talk to you for a minute?"

The grip on her arm implied she had no say in the matter. She rolled her eyes and let him drag her from the table. They

24

Chapter Three

wandered to the edge of the pier, the setting sun casting everything in an orange glow as it bled into the sea. Charlie pressed her palms into the railings, irritation rolling through her.

Jed only glared.

"What?" she asked innocently.

"You're acting like an arsehole. You do realise you have to live with this woman for twelve weeks?"

"I'm not going to pretend to be happy that I'm married to a model. A fucking *model*, Jed. God, she hasn't said an interesting thing all day."

"You haven't let her!" He crossed his arms, jacket rolled up at the sleeves to display his tattoos. "You didn't even prepare your vows."

"Because none of it is real!" Charlie shouted into the wind, her hands slapping her sides. "I didn't sign with you to pursue a career in bloody acting. You," she jabbed her finger into his chest, "put me in this position. I didn't ask for any of it."

"No." His face turned red as his hair, sweat glistening on his brow. "You just pissed off every one of your fans, and now the rest of us have to do damage control so you still have a career at all. If you didn't want to do this, maybe you should have thought about the consequences sooner."

She scoffed, turning on her heel so she no longer had to look at him. "Bullshit. All of this is fucking bullshit. It's not about my image. You just want to punish me."

"If you honestly think that, you don't know me at all." His tone fell to a gravelly rasp, his scowl leaving Charlie filled with searing acid. They'd never fought like this. It was beyond the realm of professional, but that was the problem. Jed wasn't just her manager. He was her friend.

First Comes Marriage

But he was looking at her now like he couldn't stand to be in her vicinity.

"I thought we were friends, Charlie." He shook his head. "You didn't just upset your fans. You upset me, too. I've had your back since you split from the band despite your mistakes, yet you still put everything we've built together at risk. I knew you were a livewire when I took you on, but I expected better than that."

He took a step forward. "I know that you're struggling to find yourself, but the way you are… it's going to get very lonely for you if you carry on. You might think about taking this show seriously. Taking *Tamara* seriously. It doesn't seem like she's doing this for the hell of it. It seems like she wants to find love here. You at least owe it to her to be nice."

Charlie took a long breath, her chest juddering. She hoped he didn't notice. "If you ever expected me to try to fake a marriage for entertainment value, maybe it's you who doesn't know me. This entire thing is pathetic. I want—"

The pier creaked, and a splotch of white dotted her peripheral vision. Tamara stood in front of them, her dress rippling across the wooden panels and her face pale. Something snagged in Charlie's stomach. Something she'd been trying to ignore all day. Guilt.

"Sorry to interrupt. It's just… they want us for the first dance."

"Right. Okay." Charlie shuddered in the sudden cold, glancing at Jed warily. She waited for a sign that Tamara had heard their conversation, but she only nodded with a blank expression before gathering her dress and heading back towards the party.

Jed looked at Charlie, accusation twisting sharply across his face. "If you don't want to do this, I can't force you. But I can't help you, either. At the end of the day, it's your reputation,

Chapter Three

and there's only so much the rest of us can do. It's up to you, Charlie."

He walked away, his hands in his pockets and his footfalls drowned out by the crashing waves. Charlie watched him disappear towards the glow of fairy lights and the hum of music, wondering how she'd gotten here.

And then she made her way back across the pier, decision made.

Chapter Four

Tamara pasted a false smile onto her face as she walked back into the reception, the gazebo's thin white curtains whispering in the warm breeze. After overhearing Charlie's outburst about how their wedding was pathetic and fake, the producers had caught her and asked her how she felt about her new bride. Tamara had lied for the cameras, of course. She couldn't break down now.

It wasn't as though she'd expected love at first sight. She just hadn't expected Charlie to be so blunt, so angry. As though Tamara was the worst person in the world to be married to. She'd felt that way through half of her last marriage. She couldn't do it again.

But it was too late to run away now. She wouldn't leave and let everybody think the worst. If Charlie wanted out, she'd have to do it herself.

Tamara smoothed down her lace dress, receiving a reassuring grin from Nadine. She wanted to pull her aside, tell her this was all a colossal mistake. But the cameras were still rolling,

Chapter Four

and everyone was watching, and she just couldn't handle the rejection burning brightly in her chest. So, she let her step-sister, Maria, pull her back to her seat. She was the only family member Tamara had dared invite. Her father had warned her just before the divorce that he wouldn't be paying for and sitting through another wedding, and her mother was off filming a documentary about wine in the South of France with her newest husband. Considering none of them had shown much interest in a non-televised, very real wedding the first time around, Tamara hadn't bothered to ask them. She was glad now. Though accepting of her pansexuality, Mum wouldn't be very happy to see her daughter married off to a heavily-tattooed rock star with an attitude problem.

Tamara couldn't blame her.

"So," Maria urged, wide-eyed and sparkling in her deep green dress, "how are you feeling? Ready for your first night together?" She wiggled her brows suggestively.

Tamara tried not to grimace. She had no idea what would happen after tonight. No idea where she'd even be staying. She hoped to God it wouldn't be in the same room as Charlie, though they had weeks of sharing beds and living together ahead of them. "I think we'll take some time. Get to know each other before... *that*."

"*Boring!*" Maria shouted a little bit too loudly. Her nose was bright red with sunburn, and a collection of empty champagne glasses lined the table behind her. The sweet smell clung to her breath and probably had something to do with the way she tripped over her own toes and had to lean on the back of a chair for support. "It's your wedding night and you're married to a fit rock chick! Have some rough, dirty—"

"Are we ready to cut the cake?" Nadine cut in, much to

First Comes Marriage

Tamara's relief. She squeezed Tamara's shoulders reassuringly, motioning her head to the gazebo opening. "Your bride's returned."

The sight of Charlie beneath the curtained arch made Tamara feel nauseous, and she snatched Maria's champagne to gulp it in one. Before she could even swallow, she was being pushed toward the centre of the tent, where a grand cake decorated in white roses was being wheeled in by a tuxedo-clad waiter.

It only seemed to become real at that moment. A memory hit her, too quickly: a similar three-tiered cake, only a miniature bride and groom stood on the first tier rather than the elaborate heart-shaped topper. Dominic curling his fingers around hers as they cut the cake together. Muttering, "Better not scoff too much of that if you want to keep up modelling," because he'd always made it a point to comment on how much she ate, how she'd get more jobs if she just toned up a bit, how it would be better to get "healthier" if they decided to have children.

She felt sick as the knife was placed in her hand, her fingers curling around the hilt so tightly her knuckles turned white. Charlie wore her usual blasé expression, which only made it worse. Tamara realised then that she'd just swapped one terrible marriage for another. Neither of them was real, neither of them based on real, true, healthy love.

Her eyes stung with the promise of tears.

"Shall we get this over with, then?" Charlie asked, eyeing the decorative heart with more than a little distaste.

Tamara could only nod and hope her chin wasn't as wobbly as it felt. Charlie's clammy hands, slender and covered in small tattoos, curled around her own. Her frown brushed Tamara's cheek, and Tamara tried desperately to pretend she hadn't noticed as she guided their hands towards the cake and drove

Chapter Four

the knife through the soft white sponge. A layer of lavender cream ran through, Tamara's favourite, but her stomach turned all the same. She pulled out the slice as everybody cheered, her elbow brushing Charlie's warm torso accidentally.

"Why's it purple?" she muttered in Tamara's ear.

Tamara barely heard. She was just going through the motions, trying not to throw up as she took a piece of cake and offered it to Charlie. Charlie raised an eyebrow. "What? You have to feed it to me like a dog treat as well?"

"I suppose not. It's just tradition," Tamara shrugged, already lowering the cake, but Charlie pulled her back by the wrist, eating it straight from her fingers.

Her face crumpled sourly as she chewed, a streak of lilac cream left on her lips. "What the fuck is this?" Her tongue poked out, licking away the frosting quickly. "Tastes like old ladies."

"Language, Charlie," her manager, Jed, mumbled not too far behind them.

Tamara might have laughed, but she couldn't find it in her. A line burrowed between Charlie's brows, but not before she whipped her middle finger out for Jed. "Your turn, then!"

Tamara took Charlie's piece of cake carefully. Waited for a comment. It never came.

Though tasty and soft, the cake felt dry in her mouth, and she fought a gag as she swallowed. More cheers echoed around her, the guests having formed a circle of mismatched groups in varying degrees of drunkenness.

"Yes!" Nadine clapped at the front. "Hashtag Team Tamarlie!"

Charlie's gaze still lingered as though trying to catch Tamara's unfocused one. She did her best to offer a shaky smile, for everyone else rather than her bride. *It isn't the same,* she told

First Comes Marriage

herself. She was in control this time. She wouldn't have to get her heart broken.

A voice boomed from the speakers, the DJ by the gazebo opening announcing, "All right, who's ready for the first dance?"

Charlie groaned. Tamara pursed her trembling lips. Dominic had loved the first dance. He'd chosen a song Tamara hated and had stopped swaying with her every few seconds so the press they'd invited would get a decent picture for *OK! Magazine*. When Tamara had tried to make it playful, spinning under his arm, he'd stiffened and tucked back an escaping strand of her hair.

She'd convinced herself then that it would be different behind closed doors. Dominic could be kind, loving. It wasn't all bad. But maybe she'd been a bit delusional in thinking it would ever be much better. In the end, he hadn't changed the way she'd hoped. He'd only gotten colder.

The cake was wheeled away and a soft instrumental song began playing. Tamara had never heard it before, and after the buzz of the day, the gentle, tinkling melody surprised her.

"I don't dance, by the way," Charlie said. "I'll sway at most."

"Okay." Tamara could no longer hope for anything more. It was clear this marriage was doomed to fail, and she couldn't bear to pour any more parts of herself down the drain under the guise of love.

Charlie clasped both of Tamara's hands, beginning to rock from side to side as promised. Tamara looked down, a chasm opening up inside her. But then her hands were led to Charlie's waist, and Charlie looped her arms around Tamara's neck, and it was the closest they'd been to each other all day. Whatever Jed had said to Charlie had worked. She was still in this, even if she despised it.

Chapter Four

Tamara didn't want to be married to someone who needed pep talks and punishments to behave like a decent human being. She didn't want any of this, she realised. And it was far too late to say so.

"Are you alright?" Charlie questioned finally, her brows lowering.

Tamara nodded and whispered, "Fine."

Another uncharacteristically concerned frown. Charlie angled her back away from the cluster of cameras as they danced and lowered her voice, "Look, I'm sorry about before, out on the pier, but I didn't know you'd be so serious about all this, alright?"

The apology caused Tamara's breath to hitch. She hadn't expected it. Not from someone like Charlie.

"You're not exactly what I expected, either," she replied, the barbs finally poking through her words.

"Yeah, I bet." Charlie's eyes scraped up and down Tamara's frame, dark with judgement.

Tamara sighed, shaking her head before realising people were still watching. She straightened up again quickly, resting her chin on Charlie's shoulder so that her blazer would muffle the microphone pinned to Tamara's dress. She turned her face away from the cameras. "If all you need is a bit of good publicity, I'm happy to go along with it. But I won't deal with the attitude. If you can't stand me that much, let's just stay clear of each other when we can. No more insults. No more jabs. We're happily married for the cameras, and we're strangers behind closed doors. We might have to put up with each other for twelve weeks, so we may as well use it to our advantage."

"You have it all figured out, do you?" Charlie snapped.

Anger blazed in Tamara. As though Charlie hadn't been the

First Comes Marriage

one to reject her immediately. To use Tamara in her game and throw taunts her way. She had no right to be annoyed by Tamara putting her foot down. No right to take away Tamara's final chance at what she'd hoped might have ended in love, or at least friendship. It was an effort to keep her voice to a whisper. "Do you want to do this or not? Because I have nothing left to lose from walking away right now."

"Then why are you here?"

She paused. The musky scent of Charlie's day-old perfume followed her as she pulled away. "I was here to start fresh," was all she offered.

Charlie tucked her lip beneath her teeth, contemplating. She lifted her hand from Tamara's shoulder to smooth down her short hair before returning it. "Alright. Fine. We can play up to the cameras a bit, I s'pose. I'm no actress, but my manager is one bad press article away from firing me. So, what, we're pretending we're all gooey and in love?"

Tamara tilted her head, trying to ignore the tears threatening to rise again. "Not gooey. Just... happy."

"Never been happy before. Wouldn't know how." The corner of Charlie's mouth twitched, teasing. But shadows darkened her eyes, and Tamara wondered who she was beneath it all. Beneath the attitude and the tattoos and the sarcastic jokes. Beneath the smirk and the music and the indifference. Or maybe the fame had eaten her up long ago, and she'd lost track of what parts of her were just a facade. It was easy to believe your own lies. Tamara certainly had when she'd stayed married to Dominic.

"You could start by unclenching your jaw," Tamara commented dryly, "and doing that thing where you move your lips upwards like this." She flashed her teeth quickly, forgetting for a moment that everyone watched. But their audience let out

Chapter Four

an "aw" as though Tamara had expressed her undying love, and Charlie's smirk grew to a grin.

"That's it," Tamara said.

"Right. Cheers." Charlie shuffled just a little closer, her fingers resting on the nape of Tamara's warm neck. "At least tell me this is better than your first wedding."

Tamara shrugged, ignoring the pang in her chest. "The groom liked me about as much as you do, but the cake's better this time round."

Another small smile left Tamara surprised. That she could pull any sort of reaction from Charlie was a feat in itself, even if it was for the camera's benefit. "See," she commented, "not so hard, is it?"

Charlie rolled her eyes, but she still pulled away. Still lifted her arm up for Tamara to spin under it. Something lifted in her chest as she twirled, laughing while the guests cheered and the music turned to something more upbeat.

"The cake's vile, by the way," Charlie muttered.

Tamara only laughed. If the cake was their biggest problem, it was an improvement.

Chapter Five

Charlie left the honeymoon suite as soon as the camera crew dissipated. They'd filmed the newlyweds entering the room together, an awkward ordeal where Charlie had almost tripped over the train of Tamara's dress. They'd shared a bottle of champagne over stilted conversation, and then spoken to the cameras individually about how pleased they were with their match. Tamara hated all of it. She hated lying. Hated that she couldn't see a way out of it. Hated that Charlie had another hotel room booked because she couldn't stand the thought of sharing a bed with Tamara.

As soon as she was alone, Tamara cried into her chocolate-dipped strawberries, exhausted and filled with dread. After a steaming hot shower, she wiped the fogged mirror and peered at her puffy-eyed reflection. "You can do this," she whispered. "It's only twelve weeks of your life. It doesn't mean anything in the grand scheme of things."

She'd given herself many pep talks over the years, a habit born from the first time she'd walked onto a photo shoot wearing

Chapter Five

next to nothing. But this was the first time in a long time that she'd really needed the self-assurance. She hated how vulnerable it made her feel.

By the time Nadine knocked on her door, Tamara was in her pyjamas, a honey-almond face mask on, partly to rejuvenate her sun-tired skin and partly in the hopes it would remove all tear-induced swelling and blotchiness. She was also a tad tipsy, on her fourth glass of champagne.

"Here she is," Tamara greeted upon opening the door, "the woman who talked me into all this."

"It didn't take *that* much convincing." Nadine rolled her eyes. She still wore her bridesmaid's dress, though it was crumbled and twisted around her hips, and her lipstick was a tiny bit smudged.

Tamara narrowed her eyes. "Don't tell me you've had a quickie on *my* wedding night."

Nadine shushed her, ushering her back into the suite and letting the door swing shut behind them. "I am far too classy for a quickie, thank you very much."

Tamara pointed to Nadine's earlobe. "Then *where* is your earring?"

Blushing, Nadine pinched both ears, disrupting the shimmering silver dangling from only one lobe. "Funny. They usually come as a pair. I should get a refund, shouldn't I?"

Tamara glared, her chest swelling with the same ache she'd been trying not to notice all day. Everybody else found it so easy. Swallowing the lump in her throat, she wandered back to her bed, collapsing onto the memory foam mattress and disrupting the rose petals that had been sprinkled there in the shape of the words *Mrs & Mrs*. "If I'd known you'd have one of those post-sex glows, I wouldn't have invited you up here."

First Comes Marriage

"I don't." Nadine sighed, standing in front of Tamara with her hands on her hips. "Never mind. Let's focus on you. Why don't *you* have a post-sex glow? Where's Charlie?"

"She has her own room," Tamara grumbled, rolling onto her back so she wouldn't get face cream on the pristine bedding. She plucked another strawberry from the bowl on the bedside table, licking the chocolate off slowly. "She left as soon as the cameras were turned off. Maybe I'll get lucky and she'll do a runner."

"Yes, because that will do wonders for your image. Two divorces in just over twelve months?" Nadine perched on the edge of the bed, causing the mattress to dip.

Tamara raised her eyes to glower at her upside down. "I can't force her to like me. I can't. I stopped trying to please people a long time ago, and I won't go back." Her voice thickened with tears, causing Nadine to soften.

She patted Tamara's damp hair sympathetically. "Look, we both thought that there would be a slightly more…" she debated her words, settling on, "*agreeable* person waiting at the end of the aisle, but that doesn't mean Charlie won't come round. She must be here for a reason."

"She is, and it's nothing to do with me. She just has to fix her reputation. Her manager forced her here."

"See!" Nadine threw her hands up. "You already have one thing in common."

Tamara squeezed her eyes closed, realising then that not even Nadine understood her. Understood what she wanted. Understood how much it hurt to fall out of one terrible marriage and into another.

"Oh, Tam," Nadine said with a gentle huff. "You can't forget this is television before anything else. The Cupids, the viewers,

Chapter Five

the producers... they didn't match you in the hopes you'd fall in love. They matched you in the hopes you'd make some good TV. It doesn't mean you won't ever find somebody. You will. It just... might not be here, now." She lay down beside Tamara, taking her hand. "But you will. And when the time comes, all this will be worth it."

"Who's going to want to marry me after this?" Tamara groused, tears filling her eyes.

Nadine was silent for a moment. And then, "Have I told you about my brother?"

Tamara groaned, covering her face dramatically. Nadine had tried to set Tamara up with her little brother a handful of times, even setting them up on a blind date. But Harry told pull-my-finger jokes and said things like "You're so brave, being a model," while motioning to her with his fork, as though having a body and showing it off was inspirational merely because one was fat. Slim people were never praised for it. They were just beautiful and gorgeous. They just *were*.

"See!" Nadine said. "Could be worse. You could be married to him!" She flipped over onto her stomach. "Anyway, I'm starving. Can we order room service?"

"It's almost midnight," Tamara pointed out, and didn't quite know why. The meal portions had been tiny at the reception, and her stomach felt emptier than ever. "Forget I said that," she said. "Order a bit of everything."

Nadine grinned and did just that.

Chapter Six

Tamara clutched her stomach and took a long, deep, jagged breath, the airport lights making her feel dizzy. She'd woken up at six o'clock in the morning upon the return of her midnight feast. Food poisoning was the official diagnosis from the Spanish doctor Nadine had called out. The consequence of expired chorizo in her patatas bravas.

She would have chalked it down to anxiety if she didn't feel so rotten. She still couldn't keep anything down and wasn't quite sure which end her next bout of sickness would come out. Her only saving grace was that Charlie hadn't turned up yet.

Thankfully, there were no cameras to record Tamara being stood up by her new wife in Alicante Airport. Nadine had been allowed to accompany her, demoted from the role of agent to sick-bag holder and toilet-roll supplier until they touched down in London. And as hopeful as Tamara was that all this would be over soon, that she wouldn't have to survive a two-hour flight without shitting in her expensive yoga leggings in front of a rock star, she still felt the sting. The disappointment. It crept up

Chapter Six

on her quickly as she scanned the private lounge, gaze always falling back to the entrance gate. Charlie wasn't coming.

"How are you holding up?" Nadine asked as another wave of nausea washed over Tamara. Nadine, luckily, had not eaten the chorizo, only picking at the cheese platter before they'd passed out watching the Spanish news.

Tamara only shook her head, slumping in the leather chair as a bead of sweat rolled down her forehead.

"You're right. Better not to talk. We don't want more chunks of chorizo—"

She raised a hand to silence Nadine. *"Don't* talk about chorizo."

Nadine was sensible enough to clamp her lips shut, following Tamara's gaze to the gate. "She could still come. We don't board for another," she checked her phone and winced, "three minutes."

"I hope she doesn't."

"Liar," Nadine cast her a sad smile that only made Tamara feel worse. "You know what? Forget what I said about last night. You deserve so much better than Charlie *fucking* Dean, Tammy. I mean, God, what were they thinking, matching you with a washed-up waste of space? She can't even sing that well. She just wails and does this!" She whipped her hair forward and bobbed as though in a mosh pit. Tamara might have laughed if she wasn't so ill, even if she knew Nadine was only saying it to make her feel less pathetic about being abandoned.

"I bet she'll have some serious neck problems by the time she hits forty, and then what? She'll have to play calm, boring music like, I don't know, Elton John."

Of course, Charlie fucking Dean herself appeared at the gate during Nadine's speech, wearing a dry smirk as she stopped to

First Comes Marriage

listen to the lengthy rant. "I don't mind Elton John," she chipped in, causing Nadine to jump and twist around in her seat.

"Oh!" She flashed a false smile. "Hello, Charlie. I didn't see you there." And then her eyes slipped behind her, to Jed, and Tamara was certain she turned a deeper shade of red.

"Don't stop on my account," Charlie said. Sunglasses hid her eyes, her hair mussed, shirt tucked unevenly into ripped jeans, and Tamara tried not to gag when the sharp stench of whiskey reached her. Brilliant. While Tamara had been drowning her sorrows in expired room service meals, Charlie had probably been out all night. Maybe even finding someone she actually *liked* to share a bed with.

Tamara couldn't bear the thought, and she looked away before the image burrowed into her brain and then her chest.

Jed rolled his eyes, slamming down what looked to be both of their hand luggage. "Sorry we're late.

"Looks like I'm not the only one a bit hungover this morning," Charlie said as though she was pleased, collapsing onto the seat beside Tamara.

Tamara leaned away to escape the smell, muttering, "I wish."

"Food poisoning," Nadine explained. "Terrible sickness and diar—"

"Alright, Nadine, we all know what food poisoning is!" Tamara cut in, cheeks blazing with feverish heat. She wiped her sweaty forehead with the sleeve of her cardigan, stomach beginning to churn again. Charlie shuffled away as though it was contagious.

"Will you be all right to fly?" Jed's brows furrowed with concern.

Tamara could only nod weakly, too afraid to speak. She felt like the tiniest of movements might trigger the storm in her

Chapter Six

belly.

"It was that cake," Charlie stated, upper lip curling in distaste. "You're not supposed to eat lavender. I told you. It's an omen."

"For the fate of our fake marriage?" Tamara couldn't help but quip.

Jed and Nadine raised their brows. "Come again?" Jed asked, scratching the back of his neck uncomfortably. Tamara almost rolled her eyes. Almost. She supposed they all expected her to remain hopeful and naive to Charlie's true intentions. To what this really was.

"The model and I have come to an agreement of sorts," Charlie said, tone deadpan as ever, as she leaned back and propped her ankle on the opposite knee.

"The model has a name," Tamara murmured.

"We know where we stand," Charlie added, cool as a cucumber.

Tamara wondered how she did it, how she could talk so casually about marriage. About Tamara. About their lives. Maybe Nadine was right, this wasn't about finding love. It was just about the cameras. What the viewers wanted to see. It was clear the Cupids weren't experts at all if they'd matched Charlie with Tamara, believing them to be compatible.

"So you're... faking it?" Nadine questioned.

Charlie grinned, flashing a set of pearly teeth. Not too straight, though; one of her canines jutted out slightly further than the rest. Tamara hadn't noticed that yesterday, or maybe she just hadn't been looking. "It's what everyone wants, isn't it?" She shot a pointed look Jed's way.

Jed swiped his sunglasses off and pinched the bridge of his nose. "Right. I suppose pretending is better than nothing. Does this mean you're going to actually try?"

First Comes Marriage

Charlie shrugged, swiping her arm over Tamara's shoulder and squeezing just enough that Tamara winced. "We make a pretty couple, don't we?"

Bile rose in Tamara's throat, no longer a symptom of the food poisoning. Everything really was a game to Charlie. *Tamara* was just a game to Charlie. It was as though she felt nothing at all.

Tamara nudged Charlie's arm away roughly as she stood, feeling her stomach beginning to grumble again. "I need the bathroom."

Nadine escorted her and, for once, her best friend had no wise words of encouragement to give.

* * *

"They absolutely shagged last night, you know," Charlie said, tipping her head in the direction of Jed and Nadine who sat in the seats opposite. Charlie had found them in a rather compromising position in the hotel elevator the night before, though at present, they sat pretending that they had, in fact, *not* shagged.

Tamara barely moved the entire flight, her head tipped back and eyes closed as she swallowed down deep breaths. A twinge of something foreign rippled through Charlie, and she looked away quickly as she waited for some sort of response. A hum was all she got.

"Should I be taking cover?" Charlie prodded, though they sat a fair distance from each other. Still, at the very least, Charlie's combat boots weren't safe if Tamara began to projectile vomit. Which seemed quite likely, being as she looked like a corpse.

"It isn't fair," Tamara muttered. "You go out drinking all night

44

Chapter Six

and only have a headache. I stay in my room and end up dying."

Charlie smirked, though she sensed the subtle jab beneath the words. "I was celebrating my last night of freedom."

"I think that's what hen nights are for. Not wedding nights." Tamara's fingers seemed to release slightly where they dug into the arms of the leather seat.

Charlie licked her lips, pushing again in an attempt to distract her from the sickness. "How was the honeymoon suite?"

"Wonderful. The walls are painted a lovely shade of vomit."

Charlie snorted, surprising even herself. Again. It was rare she laughed at other people's jokes, but Tamara's wit was just as dry as Charlie's, and Charlie hadn't expected it from someone like her. "Go on then. Tell me about you. What made you want to dye your hair with peroxide and stand in front of cameras all day?"

Tamara's jaw clenched. "I'm a natural blonde, thanks. And there's more to it than that. What made you want to be a judgemental arsehole and slam your guitars to shreds in front of everyone?"

Charlie froze just for a moment, though she supposed she'd earned that. She did her best to feign nonchalance, sucking in a breath through her teeth and grinning. "Ouch. She bites."

"Yeah, she…" Tamara jolted, eyes widening as her fingers rose to her lips. "She's going again."

She rose up without another word, sprinting to the bathroom at the back of the jet. Charlie grimaced when Jed and Nadine turned around. "Was it something I said?"

* * *

Tamara was quite certain she was dying, or perhaps already

First Comes Marriage

dead. She ached all over, legs cramped in the tiny bathroom after another round of emptying everything in her stomach. There wasn't much left inside her, but she still couldn't stop heaving. She wished she was home in bed, rather than somewhere over the Mediterranean. Actually, if she was wishing for things, she wished she could fly over the Bermuda Triangle and get lost forever.

She rested her head against the wall, knees tucked to her chest as she breathed through more nausea, more aching. When a timid knock at the door sounded, she didn't bother to open her eyes, supposing it would be Nadine coming to check on her. "Come in," she mumbled, struggling against her dry, sticky tongue.

But it only took the gravelly voice to realise it wasn't her best friend. "Jesus. You look rough as toast," Charlie commented.

Tamara hid her face behind her hands then. The last thing she was in the mood for was more back and forth with possibly the most obnoxious woman on the planet.

She heard a sigh, and then the door swung shut, and she thought Charlie might have left. Until something nudged her foot. "Here. Drink this. Ginger tea settles the stomach, apparently."

A steaming glass mug with a tea-bag string dangling over the handle was shoved in her face. Tamara only weighed it up warily and then pushed it away. "I can't keep anything down."

"All right." Charlie sipped the tea instead, and then her face crumpled sourly. "Fucking hell." She stuck her tongue out as though it might rid her of the flavour. "Tastes like spicy piss."

"On second thought, you've really sold it to me," Tamara deadpanned.

Charlie smirked, sliding down the wall opposite. It was

Chapter Six

cramped, their knees touching, and Tamara was too exhausted to wonder why on earth she was here at all. "I remember I had the trots for the first leg of our international tour. First time we'd gone to other countries to perform, and I couldn't stop shitting. Thought I was going to have to perform from the toilet."

"Is this your version of a pep talk?" Tamara's throat was hoarse, rough, burning.

"I don't do pep talks, love. I'm just saying, we've all been there."

More silence. Tamara didn't know what to say anymore. She kept her eyes closed, trying to focus on the gentle white noise of the plane's engine. It reminded her of being a kid again, falling asleep in the car on the way home from the zoo. If she could just stay like this.

"Nadine managed to email the producers," Charlie said. "They said they can delay our arrival until tomorrow. Put us up in a hotel until then and get a doctor to look you over again."

That, at least, brought Tamara some relief. The thought of being on camera in a couple of hours hadn't made her sickness much better. "Okay. Thanks."

Charlie seemed to shift. "You look sweaty."

"You really, really don't have to stay. I'm just going to sit here until we get ready to land."

Charlie sighed, standing up. Tamara pulled her legs closer to make room for her to leave, glad she no longer felt the weight of Charlie's presence. It didn't last long. The door swung open again a moment later, sending another jolt through Tamara's limp body. She almost groaned, desperate for the world to stop spinning just for a moment.

Something cool was pressed against her feverish forehead.

First Comes Marriage

She batted her eyes open in surprise, finding Charlie squatting in front of her, holding a cold, damp flannel to her forehead. Tamara licked her dry lips, hoping Charlie couldn't smell the sour stench of her breath as her eyes closed again without permission.

"The cameras aren't on." Tamara's attempt at a joke.

"In sickness and in health and all that," Charlie retorted, sarcasm lacing her words. But she kept holding it there, swiping away the stale sweat sitting on Tamara's temples with surprisingly delicate dabs.

Tamara would have joked about how Nadine should be taking pictures, documenting this uncharacteristically kind gesture to make their marriage seem real, but she didn't have it in her.

Charlie's touch disappeared, the cool flannel remaining as something hard was pressed to her bottom lip. "Just a sip, eh? To keep you hydrated."

Tamara winced and obeyed, the spiced tea warming her tongue and freshening her mouth. She felt it drip down her sandpaper throat and wondered how long it would stay.

"There we go," she was certain Charlie whispered.

Something new fluttered in Tamara's stomach. "Never expected a rock star like you to force tea down my throat."

"Don't worry. It'll be whiskey when we get to the hotel. Jed's treat." Another smirk as Charlie sat back with the mug, legs crossed. "I've seen enough hangovers in my time to know what to do. That's all."

Tamara could imagine that. She tilted her head as her neck began to ache, using her shoulder as a pillow. Charlie tutted and untied the black hoody hanging around her waist before folding it and cushioning her instead.

"Thanks."

Chapter Six

"Not long before we land. Think you can make it?"

Tamara only shook her head, the smell of the thick jumper curling around her. Cigarettes and woody musk, sweet lavender and crisp nutmeg. A comfort. The only scent she'd been able to tolerate without her stomach lurching since waking.

"'Kay," Charlie patted her shoulder. "Just give me a fair warning if you start puking again, will you?"

Tamara couldn't make any promises.

Chapter Seven

Charlie's usual team of ruthless paparazzi waited for them at Heathrow. She swore under her breath as though she'd forgotten who she was. It was always like this. She still went everywhere expecting peace or at least not the chaos that a mob of fans and photographers always brought.

Jed peered at her over his sunglasses warily, his way of asking: *Ready to face the music?* Charlie clenched her jaw and turned to Tamara, who had a little more colour in her cheeks since leaving the plane. She still wobbled on her feet, Nadine hovering cautiously behind her. Something tugged in Charlie's chest as her eyes widened: guilt, maybe. Whatever it was, she didn't like it. Didn't want it.

"Should we give them what they want?" Charlie asked, sizing up the crowd as they got closer to the security barrier. The first episode of *First Comes Marriage* would air that evening, and the world would already be searching to see if their relationship was genuine. She stopped, waiting for Tamara.

Chapter Seven

Tamara rooted through her handbag, hands trembling. "I don't have my sunglasses, Nadine."

Nadine only frowned. "Did you leave them at the hotel?"

"I don't know. I was trying not to lose half of my internal organs by that point."

Charlie bit her lip, taking it all in. She might have been hungover, but Tamara still looked on the verge of collapse. If the press got hold of pictures of her looking this sick, they'd come to all sorts of conclusions, none of them as simple as food poisoning. Pregnancy. Abuse. Drugs. Drink. It would follow them through the show, and probably after.

"Here." Charlie huffed and tugged her large sunnies off, handing them to Tamara along with her black Nike cap. Dark circles under Charlie Dean's eyes would be nothing new, but Tamara was a glossy, front-page model with something to lose. Nobody deserved to have their face plastered across magazines when they were feeling so unwell.

"What about you?" Tamara questioned.

"They can snap away. I look drop-dead gorgeous," Charlie flicked her non-existent hair. "You, on the other hand, look like you're just about to drop dead."

The joke won her a small smile as Tamara flattened her wild blonde hair with her cap and then covered her face with the shades. "Thanks."

Charlie extended her arm, muttering, "Shall we?"

A nod, and then they were holding hands as they continued towards the barriers. Towards the vultures. Something smug passed across Jed's face that Charlie didn't have time to decipher, but it irked her nonetheless and she dug her glare into his spine.

The flashes began before they passed through the gate. Instinct drew Charlie closer to Tamara as clawing hands and

51

First Comes Marriage

prying cameras jutted from the crowd, a narrow aisle forming under Jed's command. Thankfully, a security team kept them at bay, but it was smaller than usual. Had been since Charlie had gone solo. They were pushed and shoved like marbles being rattled around a glass bottle, and bright dots splattered across Charlie's vision. Tamara kept her head bowed beside her, clutching her handbag in one hand and Charlie's fingers tightly in the other. Her breaths were ragged, face sickly-green, and concern niggled at Charlie.

"Still with us, Hewitt?" Charlie asked.

She only hummed, steps faltering just slightly until Charlie snaked a hand around her waist instead.

"Looking comfortable, Charlie!" one pap yelled. "Is it finally time to settle down, or are you just doing it to save face?"

"Do you have anything to comment about Ghost Song's new release reaching number one?" another bellowed.

"What's it like dating a model, Charlie?"

And then, breaking the repetition, "Did Dominic give his blessing, Tamara, or are the two of you still feuding after the divorce?"

Charlie felt Tamara tense again as they waded through the voices, the bodies, Charlie fixed on Jed's leading frame.

"Does Charlie know about your history of affairs, Tamara?"

"Any comments about the rumours, Tamara? Is it true that Dominic is dating his co-star, Winter Jones?"

"Ignore them," Charlie whispered. Sweat glistened on Tamara's brow, manicured fingernails biting into Charlie's flesh now. "We're almost there."

They were. They'd managed to spill out into the cool London air, their car parked just metres away. But just as hope guttered in Charlie's chest, Tamara stumbled over a very deliberately

52

Chapter Seven

placed foot from one of the paps. A woman wearing a cruel smirk.

Anger roared through Charlie as she steadied Tamara before she could reach the ground. "What the fuck is wrong with you?" she snarled.

"Charlie!" Jed scolded.

But Charlie couldn't help it. She'd seen this woman before: the day before Charlie's split from the band. Ali French. She'd been waiting outside her hotel, and when she'd gotten nothing from that, sneaked her way in. Of course, Charlie had been wrecked that day, dragging out an after-party from the night before, making bedfellows wirh people she shouldn't. Someone had let the woman into the hotel room. The next day, a collage of pictures featuring Charlie half-naked, off her face on coke, and fooling around with her best friend's then-girlfriend had surfaced all over the internet. It had been the last straw for the band. The reason they'd asked Charlie to leave. Because her best friend also happened to be Ghost Song's drummer, Yasmin, and she'd vowed never to forgive her. Charlie didn't expect her to.

She stopped in front of the paparazzi now, that bitterness seeping into her stomach as though it had happened just yesterday. This woman had ruined her life. And now she was back, trying all over again, this time with Tamara.

So, Charlie smacked the camera out of Ali's hands and stomped on it for good measure, glad when a gaping crack split through the lens. "You're a piece of shit," she jabbed a finger towards her, ignoring the gasps echoing through the airport. "You stay the fuck away from me and you stay the fuck away from my wife."

"*Charlie!*" Jed's reprimand bellowed through the crowd, but

First Comes Marriage

she didn't care. "Get in the fucking car! *Now!*"

"You broke my camera!" Ali shrieked.

"It'll be something far worse next time, I swear to—"

"Charlie, let's go. Come on," Tamara murmured softly.

"I'll be reporting you to the police, you know!" The pap's words only spurred more fury in Charlie.

Her lip curled, fists balling, "You have some fucking nerve. I know who you are—"

"Charlie," Tamara begged, tugging her backwards with a surprising amount of force. Her eyes were pleading even through the shades. "She's not worth it. You know she isn't. Let's go."

"Listen to your bloody wife!" Jed ordered. Security began ushering them, desperate to get them out of the mob.

Shuddering, Charlie looked at Tamara a final time, and then at Ali. She kicked the camera, and it slid through the spaces between dozens of feet. "Stay away," she warned, and then she reclaimed Tamara's hand, finding it clammy and trembling. "C'mon."

"I'm going to kill you," Jed warned under his breath as he held open the door to the sedan. Charlie cast him a saccharine smile before nudging Tamara to get in and following suit. Nadine joined them, Jed taking the passenger seat in the front.

"What the fuck were you thinking?" he erupted as soon as the doors were closed.

"She was the arsehole who broke into my hotel room!" Charlie spat. "That's what I was fucking thinking."

Jed shook his head, jaw ticking wildly. "You know what, Charlie? I give up on you. I really do. You're throwing it all away, and I won't keep begging you to stop."

"She tripped me," Tamara interjected. "It wasn't Charlie's

Chapter Seven

fault. She was provoked."

"Wait, what? Are you all right?" Nadine's brows furrowed, and she leaned forward to assess Tamara. Charlie remembered when Jed used to worry about her well-being. Now, he only worried about how she looked from the outside. How much of a mess PR would have to clean up on her behalf.

Tamara slid off her sunglasses, massaging her temples. "I'm fine. Just dizzy. I wasn't expecting all that."

"None of us were," Jed grumbled, scratching his beard irritably. "Production was supposed to be keeping this all under wraps until the first episode aired. They shouldn't have known you were here."

Charlie glared out of the window, trying not to catch Jed's eye in the rearview mirror.

He sighed. "I didn't know she tripped Tamara, all right? But that's still not the way you act."

"When they invade *your* life, then you can tell me how I should act. Until then, do me a favour and shut up, Jed." Heat crawled up her neck. She couldn't do it anymore. Couldn't live like this. Maybe she acted recklessly sometimes, but she didn't deserve to have her personal space, personal life, invaded by strangers.

She was angry. Exhausted. And that made her vicious, but who else would protect her? Who else would have protected Tamara?

She thought of the questions about Dominic. The way they talked about Tamara's divorce as though they knew more about it than Tamara did. Charlie didn't believe their words, suggestions, even for a moment. They'd always make up crap, especially to belittle women. Besides, Dominic was one of those greasy arseholes who had all the charisma of a plank of wood. She'd seen him stutter his way through a Jane Austen adaptation

First Comes Marriage

once when no other TV channel had worked in her hotel room.

"How much longer are we going to do this?" Jed demanded finally.

She didn't have an answer, because she didn't know how much longer she could. She gritted her teeth instead, feeling too heavy. Too trapped. This was why she ended up going on three-night benders, partying and flitting around, trying to forget. To escape. But she had nowhere to run now. Not unless she wanted to make things even worse by abandoning Tamara and their plans.

A warmth at her fingers drew her focus away from Jed. She looked down to find Tamara's hand squeezing her own, eyes in shadow from the rim of Charlie's tattered cap. Charlie's lips parted, confused, comforted, but mostly just surprised. When was the last time anybody had handled her with... care?

She couldn't remember. Couldn't even remember the last time when everyone in the room wasn't actively fighting against her or scolding her or judging her, let alone holding her hand. Taking her side.

Charlie didn't know what to do. She pulled away, skin crawling with something unfamiliar. Something both scorching hot and icy cold. She fought down a shudder, glancing out the window again.

But Tamara's leg pressed against her own kept her feeling steady and whole, and she focused on that softness as they made their way into the city.

* * *

Tamara collapsed onto the double bed, her ears ringing and stomach aching. Flashes still zapped behind her lids, the

Chapter Seven

questions of the paparazzi echoing like a record stuck on repeat. She closed her eyes, scraping a hand over her face. Her skin didn't feel like hers. Nothing in this life did. She was used to having cameras chase after her, but a crowd like that… it made her realise just how famous Charlie Dean was. Just how little peace Tamara would be getting now that she was married to her. Even after the show, she doubted it would die down.

"You told me this would get people to stop talking about the divorce," Tamara muttered finally, sitting up to look at Nadine, who stood at the window. She was biting her nail, just as rattled as Tamara was.

"It will," she replied, a frown knitting across her brows.

Tamara shook her head. "At what bloody cost, Nadine? You've thrown me from one lion's den into another. Charlie Dean is one of the biggest names out there. Bigger than Dominic. And I'm *married* to her now. They'll never leave me alone after this."

Nadine bristled, defensive suddenly, "How was I supposed to know that someone as popular as her would sign up for the show? Reality TV is usually full of has-beens, people who aren't earning enough money from their fame anymore and need a way back in."

With a grimace, Tamara rested her back against the headboard. "Great. Thanks."

Nadine sighed patiently, softening as she perched by Tamara's feet. "I don't mean you."

"Don't you?" Tamara rubbed her pounding temples, feeling hollow and wrong, and not just because she'd thrown up a million times today. "There's no way out of this now, is there?"

"The only way out is through, as the saying goes." Nadine patted Tamara's leg sympathetically. "I'm sorry for convincing

First Comes Marriage

you to do this. I didn't know it would escalate so far. I didn't know you would be matched up with Charlie bloody Dean. But don't forget the real reason you wanted this, Tammy. To find love again."

Tamara snorted bitterly. "Somehow, I don't see that happening here."

Nadine pursed her lips, glancing around before deciding, "I'm going to nip down to the cafe. We need cake. You find something gooey for us to watch on Netflix."

"I can't eat cake," Tamara said, her stomach gurgling at the mere thought.

"I know. The cake's for me." Nadine wandered off, coming to an abrupt halt when she opened the door. Tamara saw why when she shifted, revealing a dark head of hair and an unfazed smirk.

"Jed's in my room round the corner," Charlie drawled.

Even from the bed, Tamara saw Nadine's cheeks redden. "I'm not sure why you would tell me that." She turned around to Tamara. "Weird, eh?"

Tamara only rolled her eyes, watching Nadine leave and Charlie take her place. She stepped into the suite, drumming a fist against her palm as though uncomfortable when the door swung shut behind her. "Not subtle at all, are they?"

Tamara sighed. "I suppose someone should get to enjoy themselves with all *this*," she said, waving her hand in a vague gesture.

"Is it safe to come closer?" Charlie rocked on her heels warily.

Tamara shrugged, "For now." Her throat ached and stomach was still cramping, but it felt like the worst was over. She didn't have much more to chuck up now. She was just exhausted. Anxious. Maybe a little bit afraid.

Chapter Seven

Charlie collapsed at the bottom of the bed, legs dangling over the edge and her elbow propping her up.

"What's up?" Tamara couldn't quite find a reason why Charlie would be there. Still, she couldn't help but remember the care, the tenderness, she'd shown Tamara on the plane. It had caused something to shift in Tamara. Her view of Charlie. And then she'd come to Tamara's defence in the airport, protective and furious and strong. Nobody had protected Tamara that way before. She searched for that side of Charlie now, digging past those flat eyes and terse features to the darkness shimmering beneath. It couldn't have been easy, facing mobs of people desperate to pry into her private life. Especially not if it was a regular occurrence. Tamara couldn't imagine having her life invaded so deeply. She might have been scrutinised, but she could move through the world freely. Social media was hell at times. Her Instagram captions were always being analysed to the point where she'd started to use emojis instead, but she could at least walk through an airport without being recognised. Without being ambushed.

Until now. She swallowed down the lump in her throat, the one that told her that those days were gone. She was part of this now. Part of Charlie Dean's life. They'd use her, too. Just like that paparazzi had today, tripping her up for the sake of a front page-worthy photograph.

"Jed isn't talking to me and I can't be arsed listening to his passive-aggressive huffs and puffs between PR-related phone calls anymore," Charlie explained, tracing spirals into the white bedsheets. Tamara couldn't help but follow the trail of her finger with her eyes, thinking about how, come tomorrow, they would probably have to share a bed. No more dancing around it in different hotel rooms. They'd be *married* married. Her

First Comes Marriage

stomach knotted with nerves and something else. Something hot and achy and unsettled at the thought of being that close to Charlie.

"I'm sorry that happened," Tamara said, with as much sincerity as she'd been able to offer since the vows.

Charlie's nose wrinkled. "You're the one she tripped."

"Yeah, I suppose." Tamara did her best to relax, clasping her hands on her stomach and staring at the duck-egg blue ceiling, the ornate lampshade. "I just mean it's not fair. That woman came for blood, but you're the one who becomes the enemy for reacting. Does it happen often, stuff like that?"

"Why? Preparing yourself for the flashing lights?" Charlie still teased, but something flickered beneath the mirth in her voice. It must have affected her. No sane person would be fine with what happened today. "Or is it my mood swings you're worried about?"

"Neither. I'm just saying it must be hard."

"You're famous, too."

"Not like that," she said softly, meeting Charlie's eye finally.

Charlie seemed to still, her throat bobbing, expression as unreadable as ever. A straight strand of hair fell across her lashes, ending just where a small freckle began beneath her eye. Tamara had never noticed it before.

"It comes with the job," she answered finally, lowering her gaze from Tamara to the bedsheets. "And it'll come with the wife for you. If you want to bow out—"

"Too late for that." Tamara didn't know why she answered so quickly. Why her pulse faltered like a child stumbling over a skipping rope. "They know now. They've seen us together. It wouldn't look good to give up so quickly."

"So you're stuck with me is what you're trying to say?"

Chapter Seven

Charlie's lips twitched.

Tamara couldn't help but let her own mouth curl into a smile. "Seems that way."

"Should I be worried about the affairs, then? The paparazzi thought so."

Ice washed over Tamara without warning, though she heard the jest in Charlie's voice. Still, it sent a blow to her stomach. She wanted just one person to see her as she was, no Dominic or scandal attached. She'd thought if anyone understood the way the press could twist things, it would be Charlie.

Blinking, she tried desperately to compose herself as she remembered the accusations again. The headlines. The possessiveness and the lies.

"I was only joking," Charlie said, a line forming between her brows. "Whatever happened, it's none of my business."

"No," Tamara bristled, "it isn't. It's nobody's business."

Charlie's face hardened as though offended, though Tamara couldn't imagine why. She'd been nothing but patient while Charlie acted impulsively, putting on a show and making jokes at the expense of Tamara's failed marriage.

The anger sparked in her again, and Tamara couldn't help but continue, "What about you, then? You said you knew the pap who tripped me up. How?"

Eyes shuttering, Charlie sat up and glared at the vanity. "Alright, you proved your fucking point. Do you really want to do this?"

And suddenly the thought of spending twelve weeks with this woman she didn't know left Tamara feeling raw, vulnerable, terrified. Charlie could make or break her entire career. If something happened... if they fought like this when the cameras turned on... she'd never survive the public eye. Not when

First Comes Marriage

Charlie brought so much more attention to both of them.

Her voice broke as she responded finally: "I don't want to do *any* of this."

Charlie's jaw clenched, and then her lips parted as though she wanted to say more. But she didn't, jolting as though it was a physical effort to stop herself. To keep the words in. She fidgeted with the silver wedding band around her finger, staring into the overcast sky beyond the window. "I didn't choose this either."

I didn't choose you *either*, is all Tamara heard. She bit her lip, trying not to let it affect her, but it always would.

"I didn't have any affairs," her voice wobbled as she finally admitted it. She wished she didn't still feel the need to clear her name, even now. "He was paranoid and possessive. I'd go to a party I didn't enjoy and come back to find him... *so* angry. Saying he saw photographs of me with different people. And then we'd fight all night, because he was always right, and somehow I ended up always being the one to apologise."

Silence passed between them. Tamara didn't dare look at Charlie as she continued, "I didn't have any affairs, and there is nothing that hurts me more than when they accuse me of that. I had it for two years with him, and a year after the divorce, I'm still here defending myself every day. He never had to deal with that, though I know for a fact he slept with other people when we were married. So please, don't. If we're going to do this, we need boundaries, and that's mine. No talking about Dominic."

Charlie nodded, her shoulders rising and falling with a deep breath. "Okay. I won't mention it again."

As good of an apology as Tamara knew she'd get. She accepted it by pressing her lips into a thin line and tipping her head.

Charlie licked her lips. *"If* we're doing this..." She brought her

Chapter Seven

foot up, pressing it into the knee still dangling over the bed so the rip in her jeans widened. "The cow who tripped you up at the airport has invaded my privacy before. And she's the reason my band split up. Well, the reason the band split up with me. I slept with the drummer's girlfriend, and Ali caught me in the act. Frontpage news. If, er, any of us should be accused of being unfaithful, I suppose it should be me."

Tamara sucked in a sharp breath, heart racketing against her ribs. Charlie said it as though it meant nothing. To do something like that, hurt someone you worked with every day....

"I did the shittiest thing in the world and it ruined everything." Charlie looked down at her hands, a hint of regret reaching her frown.

Tamara didn't know what to say at first. Dominic had never once shown that guilt after hurting Tamara over and over. The fact Charlie was capable of owning up to her wrongdoings... it was all Tamara could ask for. More than the small cynic in her had expected. "There *are* shittier things. Murdering someone, for instance."

Charlie guffawed as though surprised, shaking her head as her cheek dimpled. "There is that, yeah. Still, people don't often say 'it could have been worse' after committing adultery. I think I'd have a drumstick lodged in my eye if I gave that a go."

"I'm not saying I think it's right." Tamara rolled her eyes and crossed her legs. "It isn't right and it's pretty clear you know that. I'm just saying it doesn't mean you deserve to have your entire life infested by people who don't respect your privacy. Ali is still a cow. Most people get to strut around and make all the mistakes they want. It's sort of your right as a human. At least you're holding yourself accountable for what you did. Not

First Comes Marriage

many people are brave enough to do that, especially not when you're punished for it every time you go outside."

Charlie hummed as though she wasn't sure she agreed, her eyes turning absent, glossy. Tamara couldn't help but ask, "Why *did* you do it?" She'd never understood how somebody could hurt another person that way. How Dominic could have hurt *her* that way.

"I don't know why I do a lot of the shit I do," Charlie said. "I was taking a lot of drugs. Caught up in the lifestyle of it all. You always think you won't be like that when you see other celebrities off their faces, pretending ruining themselves is rock 'n' roll, but… it catches up to you. You lose yourself in it. I think I forgot how to care for a bit. I forgot the reason why I started all this to begin with. I forgot who I was."

"Do you regret it?" Tamara had to know. She had to know who she was married to. Whether Charlie could be trusted.

Finally, Charlie met her eyes. "Every fuckin' day. I might be an arsehole, but I never wanted to be a bad person. I never wanted to hurt anyone. I wish more than anything I could take it all back." She shone with sincerity, and Tamara's stomach settled with reassurance. Charlie might have been impulsive and rude and a little bit irritating, but she'd also taken care of Tamara more than once today. It had to mean something. And the way she looked now, so hollow and sombre… that was the face of someone learning from their mistakes. It's all she'd wanted from Dominic, but he'd never shown her a hint of remorse. Not even after the divorce.

She deserved a fair chance. Tamara wasn't the same person she was a couple of years ago. Charlie probably wasn't, either.

She broke away all at once, rolling up the bed to face the TV beside Tamara and plucking the remote from the pillow

Chapter Seven

between them. "Anyway. Let's see what's on the box. Reckon we made the four o'clock news?"

Tamara groaned and sank lower into the bed. "God, I don't want to know."

Charlie smirked, kicking off her boots as though she'd been invited to. Tamara didn't mind. In fact, it felt good to be closer to Charlie. Distance put barriers between them, but whenever Tamara managed to cross them, it was almost... easy. Easier, at least. It made her feel like maybe not everything had to be an act. Like maybe they could at least be civil and get to know one another.

So she let Charlie put on a documentary about aliens in Egypt, and she let the sound of her breath combined with the narrator's voice lull her into a sleep she desperately needed. And when she woke up later in the evening, dehydrated and starving and feeling a bit more like herself, Charlie was still there, brandishing room service that would be much gentler on Tamara's stomach than the chorizo had been.

It made things slightly easier to bear.

Chapter Eight

Tamara's incessant fidgeting made Charlie nervous. She tried to ignore it, watching the green hills of the British countryside roll past through the tinted windows. They were on their own now. Nadine and Jed had bid them goodbye from the hotel that morning, and this car ride was the last semblance of peace and normalcy they would have for weeks. The last time they'd truly be alone without the cameras and the other celebrities stupid enough to sign up for the show.

She chewed a loose flap of skin beside her fingernail, exhausted at just the prospect of having to do this. She had no idea what to expect, and that was usually a good thing for Charlie. She liked spontaneity and impulsiveness. But this was neither of those things. This was reality TV, and the producers would do anything to keep viewers happy. Viewers who probably didn't like Charlie much after both her stunt on stage weeks before and the betrayal against Yasmin last year.

The radio pulled her out of her worries, a familiar beat echoing around the car. Ghost Song's latest single. She glared

Chapter Eight

at the back of the driver's seat before demanding, "Turn this shite off."

He did, thank goodness, but the bitterness remained. While her band continued on without her, she was trying to save her career, married to somebody she barely knew. It was a joke. A cruel, unfunny joke.

One she deserved. It wasn't really the band she was angry at, she realised. It was herself.

Tamara's sidelong glance warmed Charlie's cheek for a moment, and she shifted her knees again. "Should we talk about how we're going to do this?"

"What do you mean?" Charlie asked.

"I mean how are we going to convince everybody that we're happily married? We need something. A plan. Like, how thick will we lay it on? Are we milking it for all it's worth or just acting casually? Because I don't know if that will be enough to—"

Charlie lifted her hands, silencing Tamara's frantic babble. "Whoa, love. Chill out."

Irritation tightened Tamara's features, and Charlie knew she'd said the wrong thing. One should never tell one's wife to "chill out." Rookie mistake.

"I'm asking you how you want to play this," Tamara said slowly, steadily.

With a sigh, Charlie weighed up her options. There were few. But she'd agreed to this mess, and she had to go through with it. In less than an hour, they'd be getting out of the car and the producers would give them their microphone packs. Cameras would watch them everywhere they went, and God knows what the other coupled stars would be like. They couldn't just hole up in their cottage and let that be that. "I suppose we'll just hold

First Comes Marriage

hands and shit."

Tamara threw her hands in the air dramatically. "It takes more than 'holding hands and shit' to make a marriage, even one that's not real!"

"Well I don't know, do I? My longest relationship was with my bloody guitar."

"I wish that surprised me." Tamara let loose a breath, resting her head against her fist. The greenery outside reflected in her eyes, shifting shades with the light. She certainly looked different from yesterday, when she'd been all makeup-free and ready to keel over. It looked like a professional had styled her, plump lips a dusty shade of pink and her hair cascading in beachy waves. Charlie hadn't made much more of an effort than she usually would, settling on her standard winged eyeliner and ripped jeans. Not even reality TV would shake her from old habits.

"Look, you don't have to worry. I'll smile and wave and look deeply into your eyes," Charlie said. "When they ask me if I'm happy with my new wife, I'll go all moon-eyed and say," she widened her eyes, lips jutting in a small pout as she emphasised her northern accent in a perfect caricature, "'I'm proper chuffed with me new bird.'"

Tamara tutted and nudged Charlie in the arm, a playful scold. "Don't you dare call me a 'bird' on national television!"

Charlie chuckled, and it came easier than she'd expected. She elbowed Tamara in the ribs softly, straining against her seatbelt to lean closer, and grabbed her hand. Tamara parted her lips in surprise when Charlie placed a gentle, dramatic kiss on her knuckles, the cold wedding ring pressing against her own mouth. "How about that? Romantic enough for you, my darling wife?"

Chapter Eight

She was certain Tamara flushed as she pulled her hand away quickly. "It's all a game to you, isn't it? You just float through life making a joke of everything."

The words dulled something in Charlie as she sat back, crossing her arms and looking out the window again. The cows looked back, chewing on grass and emitting long, droning moos. *God.* Charlie hadn't been this far from the city since adolescence, when her part-time dad used to force her on camping trips, on the rare occasion he showed up at all. How the hell would she fill her time if she couldn't play her music or go to gigs? If she was stuck in the middle of nowhere with celebrities stupid enough to sign up for this?

Tamara's words weren't true, of course. Charlie could always feel that darkness and regret simmering beneath her smirks. But it was better to be kept a secret. Better nobody else knew it was there. If she pretended not to care often enough, maybe one day it would become true. "Why shouldn't I? Why shouldn't everyone?"

Shaking her head, Tamara resumed scratching at her fresh manicure, the wedding ring glinting against the overcast daylight. "Not everyone has the luxury," she muttered. No bitterness lingered there, only something sad, something that clawed beneath Charlie's ribs as it settled in above the engine's whir.

Still, she was a creature of habit. She mimicked playing the violin sadly, mockingly, and Tamara rolled her eyes, her throat bobbing. "Forget trying to stay together until the end. I should win this bloody thing just for resisting the urge to kill you for twelve weeks."

Charlie smirked. "You could just have fun with it, you know."

"This isn't my idea of fun." Tamara's lips tugged downwards,

First Comes Marriage

and she angled away to give Charlie her back, resting her chin on her hands.

Charlie frowned, not liking the way her stomach twisted at the action. Because this *was* her trying, even if Tamara didn't realise it. She was trying to make her laugh. Trying to show her that she wouldn't kick off the moment things got tough. She was in this now. She had to be.

But Tamara didn't seem to see that, and Charlie wasn't about to force her.

* * *

Valentine's Village was bigger than Tamara had expected, the dozen or so cottages scattered among the fields with farmland yawning out for miles behind. The main house stood in the centre, which Tamara recognised as the place where the couples would usually gather for tasks, socialising, and vote-outs. Cameras greeted her the moment she stepped out of the car. She met Charlie on the other side and took it all in while the producers briefed them on what came next: meeting the other couples and then settling into their own cottage, which would include talking to the camera about their experiences so far. Then they would get stuck in with frequent visits to Cupid's Conservatory, where they would keep Sandra updated on everything. Charlie looked to be listening about as much as Tamara was, her eyes narrowed against the creeping midday sun and her posture stiff compared to what it had been just a few minutes ago. It left Tamara feeling anxious and alone until the producers gave the cue to enter the main house, a modernised home with floor-to-ceiling windows.

Charlie's hands slipped into Tamara's in a way that seemed

Chapter Eight

almost instinctive. She was grateful, even if Charlie didn't spare her a glance.

"Here we go, then," Tamara said with a wobbly smile. She squeezed Charlie's hand.

They walked over the gravel together, Tamara brushing closer whenever she stepped on an uneven stone in her tall ankle boots. But Charlie was steady, unreadable, just as she'd been at the wedding, and it left Tamara cold. They might not have fallen in love at first sight, but they'd still felt closer since the flight home. It meant she hadn't been as afraid of navigating this. Maybe they could be a team.

But she might as well have been on the other side of Charlie's glass box now.

They pushed through the door of the main house, stepping into an airy, gigantic kitchen joined with a dining room. In it, twelve people cheered, some of them vaguely familiar and others not at all.

"Welcome to the House of Love, ladies!" a dark-haired woman at the front called, sporting bright crocheted colours.

Tamara forced a smile, but Charlie didn't follow, despite all her teasing in the car. She'd grown stock-still, her eyes fixed on something, or maybe someone, Tamara couldn't recognise. She squeezed Charlie's hand again, urging her forward as they greeted the stars.

"I'm Shell!" the enthusiastic woman who had greeted them said, yanking both Tamara and Charlie into a tight hug. "And this is my new hubby, Dane! God, it's weird saying that still, isn't it?"

A looming man, muscular yet meek, with his hands tucked into the pockets of his jeans, gave Tamara a tight-lipped smile. She recognised him as one of the fitness experts who sometimes

71

First Comes Marriage

appeared on morning TV.

"I'm Tamara," she replied, "and this—"

"Charlie fucking Dean!" someone bellowed behind them. A younger lad with sandy hair shook his fingers excitedly, voice thick with an Essex accent. "How the hell've they got you on this?"

"A whole lot of begging," Charlie replied dryly, giving him a fist bump. Still, her gaze fell elsewhere, and Tamara watched carefully as she made her way around the other contestants.

She found out Shell was a soap actress, and she recognised TV presenter Rafi Hussein from a charity event last year. He was coupled up with an older celebrity chef whose cooking show Tamara watched almost every day after getting home from work, and the recognition made her dizzy.

She noticed that the contestants' reactions to Charlie weren't quite as warm as they made their way around the group. Some seemed too shocked, or perhaps intimidated, to greet her, and others laughed nervously. She really didn't belong here. She was an A-lister, a lion in a room of tabby cats. Tamara hadn't thought about her fame too much before, but she couldn't help but want to shrink. Did people wonder why someone like Charlie had been matched with her?

"Aren't you going to say hello to me?" a gravelly voice enquired as they reached the back of the group. It came from a woman with black and sea-blue hair and piercings: someone who looked more compatible with Charlie.

Or perhaps not. A ripple ran through Charlie as she pursed her lips impatiently and tipped her head. "Sloan. Fancy seeing you here."

"Fancy that."

Tamara didn't like the way Sloan raked her eyes up and down

Chapter Eight

Charlie predatorily. It left a bad taste in her mouth, and the thick silence draping over them like heavy velvet made her feel as though everybody else knew something she didn't.

"Is this your wife?" Sloan continued, her attention falling on Tamara. Mischief flashed across her face. "You like your models, don't you?"

Charlie's grip on Tamara's hand tightened, shoulders bunching with tension. Anxiety knotted in Tamara's stomach as she assessed them both, suffocated by the unexpected tension. She was too aware of the gazes on them, and the cameras. Too aware that the last time Charlie had felt so stiff, she smashed a paparazzi's camera.

"I'm Tamara," she said in an attempt to dissolve the strange atmosphere, extending her hand.

"I know who you are, lovely." The kind word was acidic, wrong, but Sloan shook Tamara's hand anyway. "I've seen you in *Vogue*. I was more accustomed to Page 3 back in the day. I suppose that's a step up for you, Charlie."

Page 3 had already been banned by the time Tamara made it into the industry. It was clear Sloan had a few years on Tamara, though her skin still glowed, her figure full in all the right places the way lingerie companies loved with their models. Companies that would never hire Tamara and her perfectly healthy wobbly bits.

Charlie tugged Tamara closer without warning, rough and perhaps a bit possessive, though she wasn't staking her claim. More showing her off. Using her. As though Sloan was an ex and Charlie wanted to rub something in.

"Certainly is, Sloan," Charlie uttered tactlessly, moving on to the woman beside Sloan. She was quiet, probably as uncomfortable as Tamara, her hands clasped in front of her

First Comes Marriage

and her eyes large behind thick-framed glasses. "You must be the missus. Good luck, love."

"*Charlie!*" Tamara muttered, though she was surprised it had taken this long for Charlie to piss someone off.

"Don't be like that, Chaz," Sloan said with a careful smirk. "You liked me once."

"*Once* being the operative word. It lasted all of a night. Aren't you going to introduce me to your wife?"

"Ella," the woman said, her thick red braid falling over one shoulder. "I'm a vlogger. I must say, I'm a huge fan of your music, Charlie. I used to have posters of you in my bedroom."

"Blimey." Charlie chuckled and rocked on her heels. "That's not something you should go around admitting." Still, she gave a charming wink as though appeasing a fan.

Tamara rolled her shoulders back, feeling uncomfortable in her own skin around so many strangers. "We should go and get settled in our cottage."

Nodding, Charlie flashed Sloan a final look, perhaps a warning, before tugging Tamara away. The cameras followed them, meaning Tamara never quite got the opportunity to ask who Sloan was. Instead, that strange, shivery tension festered as she spoke to the cameras about first impressions and loaded her clothes into a shared wardrobe: pristine pastel blazers clashing with Charlie's frayed denim.

She couldn't help but wonder, once again, what on earth she'd gotten herself into.

Chapter Nine

A t the very least, Charlie had hoped this might be the perfect escape from any reminders of the band and her dwindling reputation in the industry, but Sloan Simpson's presence proved it was the opposite. She'd been stitched up. Forced into a house with the woman who had been the catalyst for everything bad that had happened in Charlie's life.

The woman she had been in bed with the night Ali French broke into her hotel. The woman Charlie had fucked, knowing very well she was dating her best friend at the time, because she'd been too arrogant and too wasted to care.

As soon as she got a spare minute, Charlie rushed into the bathroom of their cottage, the only place with no cameras. She splashed punishingly cold water over her face—again, again, again—too rattled to look at herself in the mirror. It had taken a long time to stop hating herself for sleeping with Sloan. Maybe she never had.

She clutched the edges of the sink until her knuckles turned

First Comes Marriage

white, wishing she could call Jed. But he'd taken her phone this morning, just as Nadine had Tamara's—the rules of the show. No contact with the outside world. So, she had two options: walk out now, ruin her deal with Tamara and say goodbye to fixing her mistakes in the process, or stay here with a woman who only served as a reminder of every awful thing she'd ever done.

"Charlie?" A gentle tap sounded on the door.

"What?" Charlie bit, and instantly regretted it. It wasn't Tamara's fault, and she certainly hadn't signed up for all of Charlie's baggage. The more Charlie learned of her, the more she wondered why Tamara was here at all. She was too... hopeful. Uncorrupted by the concept of reality TV and fame. She'd been burned before and yet she was still here for a second marriage and genuinely wanted to make it work, at least for the duration of the show.

And Charlie was the complete opposite: dysfunctional, non-committal, and a terrible, cynical fuck-up.

"I just wanted to make sure you were okay," Tamara said, her voice quieter now. Wounded. "I'll carry on unpacking, though. Give you some space."

Charlie's heart clenched and she didn't know why. She only knew she felt heavier, sicker, when Tamara's retreating footsteps turned to silence and she was left alone again. With a huff, she dried her face on a fluffy, lemon-scented towel and then crossed the hallway to the only bedroom in the cottage. Tamara had her back turned as she hung pretty floral dresses and well-ironed blouses in the walk-in wardrobe, her face reflected in the tall mirrors spanning the sliding doors. Her cheeks were rosy and her eyes bloodshot. Guilt scratched its claws through Charlie's insides. It felt like all she'd done since

76

Chapter Nine

meeting Tamara was disappoint her. Usually, not something she bothered to feel bad about. It was so common that she'd learned to block it all out, regardless of who it came from: Jed, her publicist, her fans. Since the band's split, she'd put everybody into a box, learned to pack them away and distance herself. But Tamara....

She didn't know why it felt different with Tamara, a woman she barely knew.

Charlie perched on the bed, where matching *hers* and *hers* robes were folded with *#FirstComesMarriage2023* embroidered in pink on the lapels.

"Do you think you brought enough clothes?" She directed the remark at the overflowing suitcases Tamara was still pulling clothes out of.

Tamara let out a mirthless gust of breath, a laugh that had decided to halt at the last minute.

"Look..." Charlie tried again, clasping her unsteady hands together. "I didn't know she'd be here. If I did... there's no way I'd have signed up for this bullshit."

"She's an ex?" Tamara pretended to be more interested in folding her jeans, but curiosity sharpened her voice nonetheless.

The innocent question took Charlie aback. She'd forgotten that not everybody knew her life story. Not everybody knew all of her mistakes, the skeletons she wanted so badly to bury. "Not quite. She's the woman I told you about. The one I slept with when she was dating my bandmate. I suppose this is my karma."

Finally, Tamara turned around, softening until Charlie couldn't look at her. She was so bloody gentle, calm, understanding. All the things Charlie could never be. All the things she'd never been surrounded by before.

First Comes Marriage

Charlie scraped her hair back and began pacing, kicking the wheels of her own abandoned suitcase in annoyance. "They knew what they were doing when they put us both here. It's so fucked up. All of this. They don't care about us. They just want to make good TV, don't they? Nobody cares. Not even...." Not even Jed. Not even her old bandmates. Nobody in the world cared about the regret, the self-loathing, that being trapped here with Sloan dredged up. Her job was to perform. Be a rock star, be edgy, be loud, but don't get cocky or angry or too drunk. Make good music, but water down the lyrics, the feeling, in case it's too much for the listeners. Keep her personal life private, but let the press invade her hotels and her home, dragging up every piece of her they could so it was front page news. And she was just supposed to accept it. She was just supposed to live with being a commodity. She'd been one for so long she'd forgotten what being a person felt like.

Maybe a self-destructive part of her had wanted to test the boundaries the night she slept with Sloan. Maybe it had been an unconscious way of destroying a life that wasn't hers. Taking back control. Saying, *You want a show? I'll give you one!* This life was fucking her up, so she'd made it even by fucking up life right back.

"I know," Tamara whispered, a sympathetic line forming between her brows. "It's cruel, the way everyone tries to pick you apart. I know, Charlie."

"I never wanted to see her again," Charlie admitted, dragging her tongue across her dry bottom lip. "I hate myself for what I did. It's the biggest mistake I've ever made, and I just... I didn't need the walking fucking reminder strutting around here, smirking at me like she's enjoying it."

"So what do you want to do?" Tamara sat on the bed,

Chapter Nine

looking up at Charlie. There was no judgement there, no anger, though she had every right to it. "If you want to call it quits, I understand."

Charlie stopped, frozen. It was the last response she'd expected. Tamara should have been telling her to pull herself together, to grow up, to get on with it because she didn't have a choice. "I thought you needed all this as much as I did."

Tamara shook her head. "I didn't think it would be like this. They're playing with our *lives,* for God's sake. If it were me, if they brought in Dominic or someone from my past… I'd feel the same. I'd be angry, too. And I'd want to leave."

Their knees brushed as Charlie fell onto the bed beside her, scraping a hand across her face and resting her elbows on her thighs. She did want to leave. But where would she go? She was hanging onto her career by a thread, and she had no one waiting for her on the outside to tell her they understood, that she did the right thing. Only angry managers and publicists and nasty headlines and bandmates who wanted nothing to do with her.

"Doesn't matter where I go," she admitted, clasping her hands against her mouth so the words were muffled. "Whether I'm here or not… I'm so fucking sick of it, Tamara." *I'm so fucking sick of myself.* She'd never admitted it before, not to anyone. But it didn't feel like a mistake. It felt like lifting a weight off her back.

The mattress shifted as Tamara leaned closer, holding Charlie's arm and squeezing carefully. "We're a team now. If you want to stay, I've got your back. You're not in it alone. And if you want to go, we'll walk away together."

Charlie looked down at the ring on her finger, something strange fluttering inside her hollow chest. After a long, steady

First Comes Marriage

breath, she placed her hand over Tamara's and tried not to notice the black speck in the corner of the room. The camera.

Despite its presence, she believed Tamara, so she straightened up, still holding her hand, searching her features. Pretty. She was so pretty, all apple cheeks and dimples. Her eyes were piercing in their sincerity. More trustworthy than any Charlie had seen before. She found herself focused on Tamara's plump lips, her slight overbite leaving her teeth slightly visible even when she wasn't smiling. Even when she was just looking at Charlie, waiting, wondering.

"You really want to be dragged into all my shite, Hewitt?" Charlie asked.

Tamara shrugged. "It's a bit late for that. I already said '*I do.*'"

A smirk broke free on Charlie's face, the pad of her thumb drawing circles along Tamara's hand as though desperate for any friction. She didn't understand any of it, and maybe it was better that way. Maybe she just wanted whatever Tamara was offering, because she sure as hell didn't deserve it, and Tamara would figure that out sooner or later.

"I suppose I'll get unpacking then," she decided. And she didn't know why she did it, why she brought Tamara's hand to her mouth and left a quick kiss there. A hint of coconutty hand wash clung to her soft skin. Charlie burned with embarrassment as she stood up, distracting herself with her black suitcase. Tamara said nothing, only went back to hanging her clothes.

As though it hadn't happened at all. Or maybe just as though it was something that didn't need to be questioned. They were married, after all. Charlie was allowed to kiss her wife.

She just hadn't expected to want to.

* * *

Chapter Nine

Tamara had been roped into slicing up potatoes by a very enthusiastic Shell. Every so often, Alessandro, the TV chef and Rafi's new husband, would wander by from his fancy duck confit to tell her she needed to cut them thinner or add seasoning, which had started off nice but now was getting quite annoying. Charlie, of course, had been put on cocktail duty, which mostly seemed to involve drinking the alcohol straight from the bottle and had a surprisingly small amount of mixing involved. Thankfully, Sloan had disappeared. Tamara didn't like the woman even a little bit. The way she jeered and tried to push Charlie's buttons. The way she looked at Tamara as though she found something funny. And perhaps just a little part of Tamara was afraid Charlie might be tempted. She clearly had been before, and Sloan was much more Charlie's type with the tattoos and colourful hair and carefree attitude. They made sense.

Tamara and Charlie didn't.

She rubbed her sternum absently, pretending to be interested in Shell's conversation. "Jack has already said he wants to swap wives. Can you believe it? I think some people are just here for their five minutes of fame."

Humming, she eyed Jack, the Essex reality star who was paired with a bubbly Scottish girl group member named Gabby who had starred on *The X Factor* a couple of years ago. Tamara believed Shell's claim when she found him trying to start a cocoa powder fight with Ella. Ella didn't seem too upset to be receiving his attention, either. Maybe Tamara really had misunderstood the entire premise of the show. But why were people so eager to get married if they didn't intend to at least *try* to make it work? Didn't they know how difficult divorce was?

First Comes Marriage

"How about you? You and Charlie seem pretty strong. I'm surprised, actually. I've heard…." Shell winced, knife growing wobbly in her hand as she tried to chop the shallots. "Well, I'm sure you know what everyone's heard. And with Sloan being here—"

"Charlie's made it clear that she's ready to move on from her past," Tamara replied steadily, hoping her own doubts didn't make her voice wobble too much. "We're enjoying ourselves. So far, so good."

"But do you think she's here for love? Because I've heard she's a bit of a player. She's slept with a lot of women. Y'know, she's a rock star. She doesn't seem like the marrying type, even if it is reality TV."

Tamara hesitated. "People can change." Still, she wondered just how much of it was true. She hadn't seen much of "rock star" Charlie Dean since the incident in the airport yesterday, and before that, the wedding. It wasn't as though she'd hidden her history with Sloan or hadn't owned up to mistakes she'd made in the past. But was that because Tamara was just someone to vent to, or because she wanted Tamara to trust her? She didn't know, and the last thing she needed was another spouse she couldn't trust.

"Yeah but… *that* much?" Shell asked, wincing as though it was far too big an ask.

Tamara bit her lip, dusting potato peel off her hands. She couldn't help but glance at the nearest camera stationed above them before looking away just as quickly. It was odd having to be so careful of what she said, knowing every movement was recorded. Heard. The microphone pack taped to the base of her spine proved that.

"It's early days," she decided, "but she hasn't given me a reason

Chapter Nine

to doubt her." If nothing else, Charlie was painfully blunt.

"Bet you didn't expect to get matched with her. She's the furthest person from Dominic Lowell you could get, eh?" Shell giggled, teasing, but hearing his name left Tamara feeling cold. Shell seemed not to notice. "Tell you what, if I were married to him, I'd beg for him back on my hands and knees. That man is so dreamy."

You should be begging for me to take you back, Dominic had said the night Tamara had decided it was time for the divorce. *Who do you think you are?*

She knew now that she deserved better than those words. Deserved better than to be belittled. She deserved apologies. She deserved to be fought for. And while she'd come to see that, nobody else did. Dominic would always be the charming hero of her tragedy. And she would always be the fool who let him go.

A gag sliced through their conversation, through Tamara's involuntary silence. Charlie shuffled between them, sticking her tongue out in distaste. "I'm a lesbian, and even I know there are better blokes than him out there. He's very... hairy."

Shell turned the same shade of red as the bell pepper she'd been chopping, wiping her hands uncomfortably on a tea towel. "I didn't mean—"

"Your *hubby* was looking for you in the dining room." Charlie patted Shell's shoulder, a hint of acidity in her voice. "I'll take over there if you want."

"Oh. Okay. Thanks." With a false smile, Shell disappeared.

Tamara sucked in a deep sigh and continued slicing, her face blazing until she tucked her chin into her chest.

"You alright?" Charlie asked, making a pig's ear of Shell's halved peppers so that seeds and juice sprayed all over the

First Comes Marriage

chopping board.

"Everyone thinks they already know us," Tamara said quietly, trying to swallow down the lump in her throat.

"Yeah, well, that's because they're all fucking boring."

"Charlie." She rolled her eyes, half-scolding and half-wishing she could laugh with her. These weren't her people, and they certainly weren't Charlie's. Half of them were here to put on a good show and gossip, and the others probably had no better work scheduled. Most of them would be divorced in a month's time. It was a shame, but so far, it seemed to be the truth. It never seemed that way on TV. The couples always seemed so happy. Maybe they were just like Tamara and Charlie: liars.

"They are!" Charlie defended. "They have nothing better to do than talk about shit they've read on Twitter. And if they fancy that ex of yours... well, there's no hope for them. He's a prick."

This would be aired on TV. Tamara wanted to shrink and die. But she was right. Dominic was too good at charming the world. Nobody knew how cruel he could be behind closed doors.

She bowed her head, unwilling to entertain anything that would surely backfire on her later.

"You don't have to put up with it, you know," Charlie commented, warming Tamara's face with a sidelong glance. "You're allowed to stand up for yourself."

"Maybe I'm tired of having to," Tamara mumbled. "I know when to pick my battles, Charlie."

Charlie placed the knife down, leaning against the counter to face Tamara properly. Her hazel eyes were scrutinising and full of dancing shadows. But she only hummed, her mouth tipping with something that looked like pride. "A talent I never quite

Chapter Nine

learned."

Tamara shrugged, defences melting in an instant. She understood. Every time she let someone believe the worst in her, it was a choice. She'd spent too long trying to prove herself, but she only needed her own approval now. Charlie's reactions seemed more instinctive, maybe because she hadn't yet gotten there or maybe because nobody had ever told her it was okay to save her energy for more important things and people.

So, playfully, she nudged Charlie and said, "Maybe I can teach you."

"Maybe you can," Charlie agreed. "I'll warn you, though: I'm a handful. Failed all my classes in college."

Tamara hummed. "I believe it."

Chapter Ten

Of course Sloan chose the seat directly opposite Charlie and Tamara at the dinner table. She shot Charlie an innocent, saccharine smile as she sat, which Charlie ignored by feigning interest in Tamara's conversation with the bubbly soap actress who Charlie had been attempting to stay clear of. Shell, was it? Next, she'd be meeting somebody named Sand or Conch.

"We should play a game to get to know one another better," Ella suggested beside Sloan, voice high-pitched with excitement.

"Or we could just eat our tea," Charlie quipped, thanking Alessandro as he served her a fancy plate of lettuce, prawn, and avocado. It smelled awfully vinegary, stinging her nostrils as it wafted past her onto her placemat. She'd heard plenty of hype around the TV chef's Soho restaurants, but if all the portions were this small and healthy, she'd rather go to KFC.

"This is a three-course meal, darling. Don't call it *'tea,'*" Alessandro muttered before heading back into the kitchen to

Chapter Ten

bring out the rest of the plates.

Charlie raised an eyebrow, turning to find Tamara already stifling a laugh through pursed lips. It left Charlie smirking too as she speared a pink, lemony prawn and then abandoned it, opting for her beer instead.

"I think a game is a sick idea," Jack chimed in from the other end of the table. "What about Never Have I Ever?"

"*Jesus,*" Charlie muttered, "how old are you lot? Ten?"

"I've never played that one," Ella replied, pushing her glasses up the bridge of her nose. The confession earned a few gasps, which left Charlie rolling her eyes.

"Sorted, then. Let's do it," said Jack.

"I don't think—" Rafi's protest was swiftly cut off by Jack.

"Never have I ever..." he rubbed his hands together as though warming them by a fire, looking around the table slowly, "fondled a bird in the supermarket."

Charlie almost choked on her beer.

"Does he mean like a chicken drumstick?" Ella questioned.

"I just think it's so disrespectful to call women '*birds,*'" Shell had already begun ranting. Dane nodded beside her, feigning understanding while also sipping his drink. Charlie couldn't make out if he'd forgotten they were playing, but he certainly looked the type to feel up women in the middle of Waitrose.

Meanwhile, Rafi was murmuring, "This is a bit too heterosexual for my tastes."

Charlie was certain she could feel her brain cells decaying as she listened to the five different conversations and finally risked a prawn. Tamara shook her head, amusement still curving her lips. Her foot nudged Charlie's as though saying *I'm with you*, and Charlie couldn't help but grin as she finally laughed. It was musical, not as loud as the other voices vying for attention, but

First Comes Marriage

loud enough to soothe the chaos just slightly. Loud enough that Charlie got a bit lost in it for a moment. It occurred to her that she'd never really heard Tamara laugh before. She wanted to hear it again.

"Let me go!" Jack's wife, Gabby, piped up. Charlie was certain she was already on her fifth glass of wine. She swayed plenty in her seat, anyway. "Never have I ever gotten a piercing on my private parts!"

"Jesus Christ," Tamara muttered around a piece of lettuce.

Sloan's sultry voice emerged from the chaos with, "How private are we talking?"

Of course Charlie chose that exact moment to lift her gaze and ended up making eye contact. Sloan winked as though Charlie knew the answer. As though Charlie remembered that night at all. Beside her, Tamara stiffened, and somehow it only left Charlie feeling worse. That Sloan had the audacity to keep trying to air their dirty laundry in front of Charlie's wife, whether real or not, disgusted her.

"Don't put me off my food," Charlie groused, scowling before stabbing through her pickled salad again.

"You weren't too put off when you saw it," Sloan drawled, taking a long sip of white wine. "What about you, Tara? Any hidden piercings?"

Tamara straightened up, folding her hands in her lap as she gazed at Sloan coolly. For once, Charlie had no real idea of what she was thinking. "My name's Tamara. And I suppose that's for my wife to find out, isn't it?"

The bite to her words surprised Charlie — impressed her, even. She grinned proudly, but it soon ebbed when Sloan said, "Oh, so you haven't slept together yet? Must have been a boring wedding night."

Chapter Ten

Tamara didn't miss a beat, as though she'd already expected the retort. "We're taking things at our own pace. It doesn't stop us from having fun."

"Well, be careful. Charlie gets bored *very* easily."

Charlie gritted her teeth, her skin prickling with anger as she sought Tamara's hand. It was waiting for her, open in her lap beneath the table. Clammy and trembling just slightly. The fact drove Charlie's defences to rise. "Don't—"

But before she could warn Sloan, Tamara cut in, "In your experience, perhaps. I think I'll do just fine at keeping Charlie interested. Don't you?"

Jesus. It was a better retort than Charlie could ever expect, and she whipped her head around in surprise. Tamara's features were sharp, cutting, as they fixed on Sloan across the table. Arrogant, even. Heat stirred deep in Charlie, one she hadn't felt for a long, long time. One that tugged towards Tamara. *Attraction.* Tamara was standing up for both of them, pissing Sloan off, and... well, it was enough to turn Charlie on. She hadn't expected that fierceness in such a soft woman. Maybe she'd underestimated Tamara in more ways than she'd known.

Sloan's eyes flickered with something. A blade glinting in the light. She didn't pry her gaze away as she spoke up. "I've got one. Never have I ever slept with my best friend's partner."

Charlie hissed in warning as the atmosphere dulled, the conversations trailing off. She ignored the roomful of stares, focusing only on Sloan. They probably already knew. *Everybody* knew.

"Er..." Ella muttered, shifting uncomfortably. "Sloan, maybe you shouldn't."

But Sloan wasn't deterred. "Drink up, Charlie."

Charlie's pulse echoed in her ears. Tamara's grip got tighter,

First Comes Marriage

warmer, her body angling closer to Charlie as though shielding her. But it wasn't enough. None of it was enough.

"Am I so unforgettable that you can't just drop it?" Charlie snarled finally.

"Everybody in this room knows that you're not here for love," Sloan replied, tipping her head haughtily. "You're here because you're a drunken mess who can't sell records anymore, and this is the only way you can stay relevant. And even if that wasn't true, marrying a fucking clean-cut model like her? The only interesting thing about her is her ex-husband."

A deafening screech of Charlie's chair legs rent through the dining room as she stood, leaning forward with her fists digging into the table. "Don't bring everyone else into your fucking games!"

"*Charlie*," Tamara begged, clutching her arm to hold her back, but the damage had been done. "Don't. Please."

Charlie trembled with rage as she continued, "You don't know anything about either of us. Considering the fact you haven't paid even a little bit of attention to your wife since I got here, you might want to focus on your own shitty marriage before you start worrying about mine. You want to talk about relevance? How many arenas have you sold out?"

"She's not worth it," Tamara whispered over and over, "she's not worth it. Walk away." Her voice seeped through the white-hot fury, reminding Charlie of where she was. Who was watching. This would all be televised, and if she lost it….

Her career would be over. She was beginning to wonder if someone had handpicked Sloan for that purpose entirely.

"Come on, Charlie," Tamara said. "Walk away."

Charlie didn't look at their audience before snatching her arm from Tamara and marching off. She didn't look back, but she

Chapter Ten

heard Tamara's heels clicking behind her, following. Charlie burst outside first, for once glad for the fresh, clean air and the soft grass beneath her feet. It was easier to come back to reality here. Easier to catch her breath if she just stared at one cloud floating in the twilight.

The door swung again, and then Tamara was in front of her. A frown wrinkled her forehead, but it didn't seem to hold any annoyance. Only concern. She cupped Charlie's jaw in her hands, forcing her to meet Tamara's eye. "You're a better person than her. Don't let her lower you to her level."

Glaring, Charlie looked down, rooting through her pockets for a cigarette. She'd been trying to cut down if only for the sake of Tamara, doubting the model would want to share close proximity to someone who always reeked of smoke, but she needed it now. She plucked one into her mouth, lighting it with her hands cupped around the orange glow until it caught. And then she took a long drag, closing her eyes as Tamara stood back, waiting.

"She's here to mess with me," Charlie grumbled. "I fucking know she is."

"So don't let her. You were right. She's barely looked at Ella, and people will see that. But if all she wants is a reaction, you need to stop giving her one."

"It's not that fucking easy!" She toed the loose soil, a desperate attempt to use her excess energy on something other than Sloan's smug little face. God, Charlie was so tired of it. So tired of everything. She didn't know how to escape anymore. Didn't know how to escape what she'd done. Didn't know how to escape herself. "I'm not just going to stand back and let her say shit about us. I won't, Tamara. It's not who I am."

"I know that." Tamara crossed her bare arms over her belted

91

First Comes Marriage

dress, eyes glistening in the mild breeze. "I know. I'm sorry."

Charlie took another drag, the smoke curling around both of them. Tamara didn't flinch; she just kept watching Charlie steadily as though she had all the patience in the world. As though Sloan's words hadn't affected her at all.

"How can you just stand there and let her say that shit about you?"

Tamara shook her head slowly. "I'm a plus-size model, Charlie. Do you think she's the first person to say something nasty about me? She won't be the last, either. I don't care what she thinks about me. After we're done with this show, I'll never have to see her again, but I'll still have to live with myself. If I spend any more of my life hating who I am because I believe things that other people say or getting angry because not everybody likes me, I'll never be happy. And that's all I want. To be happy."

Charlie paused at that, finally looking at Tamara properly as she stubbed out her cigarette. If she had half of that strength, that patience... But Charlie had given up on *happy* a long time ago, perhaps even without knowing it. She wasn't striving for anything but to just get through the day. There was no end goal, no way out. Only survival. And to survive, she had to defend. She had to make sure nobody tried to hurt her.

And she'd carried that coping mechanism here with her.

"If you're right about Sloan, and I think you are, she won't stop," Tamara continued, breaking the sudden silence. "So you can get angry and throw a tantrum and walk away now or you can piss her off even more by ignoring her. You have to choose how much of your energy she's worth."

Her gaze slid past Charlie, wariness filling her expression. Charlie turned, finding a silhouette through the tall windows.

Chapter Ten

Her hackles rose immediately, until the door opened and Rafi stepped out, scratching his dark beard roughly. "I was just coming to check on the two of you. She's a handful, isn't she?"

"That's one word for it," said Charlie stonily.

"Look, keep your heads up." He patted Tamara on the shoulder, mouth downturned with sympathy. "It's tough, but the way you two are sticking together... well, I didn't expect it. You might be like chalk and cheese, but you've got something good. I've been waiting my entire life to find someone who'd be as quick to defend me at a dinner table as you two were tonight. Almost brought a tear to my eye." He mimicked wiping a tear from his cheek, dragging a mangled chuckle from Tamara. Like one domino falling into another, Charlie couldn't help but join in. Still, something warm flared in her. Tamara *had* defended her, and Charlie hadn't thought twice about doing the same, so spurred by the anger Sloan had caused. Just a few days ago, she'd made assumptions about Tamara just because she and Sloan shared the same occupation. Now, hearing somebody else say them... Tamara deserved better than that. They were two entirely different people. She should have been running the other way by now, but she was still here. Still standing beside Charlie.

"Thank you, Rafi," Tamara embraced the TV presenter. "We're doing our best. It's good to have at least one friend here."

"Oh, you're welcome to pop round our cottage any time," Rafi said, rubbing Tamara's back. "No, really. Alessandro keeps trying to teach me how to cook, and I can't keep pretending to be interested in basil."

They both laughed again. Tamara stepped back, her hand falling straight into Charlie's. The instinct of it caused Charlie's breath to hitch, even as she twined her fingers through Tamara's

First Comes Marriage

and shuffled slightly closer. She eyed the camera by the door, unable to help but wonder if it was just for the two of them. But considering their most intimate moments had taken place without cameras at all, maybe....

Well, maybe it was more real than they'd ever planned for. Not that Charlie knew what *it* was. She only knew she liked having Tamara around. Liked being close to her. Liked seeing her smile. She liked having somebody on her side.

"You know, Charlie," Rafi continued, "I must say I'm surprised. I thought you'd be awful, but you seem to be treating Tamara well. Married life must be taming you."

"I'm not ready to become a good little housewife just yet," Charlie retorted, teasing, "but thanks, I think. I kind of thought you'd be awful too, but compared to some of the people in there, you're alright."

"No, I am awful." He winked. "But seriously, guys. Take no notice of Sloan. She'll get her comeuppance. Just focus on the *loooove.*" He sang the last word as though they were all five years old, which Charlie should have hated. But he'd made a special effort to show his support, and that was something Charlie didn't have often.

"I've dealt with plenty of Sloans," Tamara said. "We can handle her."

We again. Like they really were a team.

"And you're... okay with all the history?" Rafi's eyes darted, unsure, to Charlie as though she was no longer part of the conversation. Perhaps she'd changed her mind about him after all.

Tamara shrugged. "Charlie has been honest with me about her past, and I've been honest with her about mine. It's all I can ask for."

Chapter Ten

"Everybody has baggage," Charlie added, even if hers was heavier than most. So heavy she probably wouldn't be allowed through customs with it. "Mine just happens to be plastered on front pages."

"Well, I suppose now is your chance to redeem yourself." Rafi squeezed her shoulder gently and then took a long breath. "Well, I better get back to Alessandro. He's very stressed about the duck, and apparently, as a supportive husband, I must nod and soothe him as required."

"Good luck," Tamara smiled.

Charlie only tipped her head. "See ya."

And then it was just the two of them. Charlie faced Tamara carefully.

"Feeling better?" Tamara asked.

"I'm not going back in there." Charlie's jaw clenched with defiance. She hadn't realised how close they were standing now. Close enough that she spotted a tiny smudge of lipstick on Tamara's chin.

"That's okay. I don't want to either. Let's just go home and stick one of those weird alien documentaries on."

It wouldn't be that easy. Charlie would probably be summoned to Cupid's Conservatory soon. The producers had briefed them that they'd usually have to talk to Sandra once a day to give her and the viewers a personal insight into their relationships and the goings on within the show. Sandra was usually the one to listen, offering advice and asking questions.

But going home—a word she never thought she'd use here, let alone anywhere else—sounded a good plan until the time came, so she let Tamara lead her back to their cottage. To home.

Not without first asking, "*Do* you have any secret piercings?"

Tamara scoffed. "Not telling," she replied, as though she

95

wanted Charlie's imagination to run wild. Which it most certainly did for the rest of the night.

Chapter Eleven

"That shower lasted longer than my dad's last marriage," were the words Tamara was greeted by as she emerged from the bathroom in a cloud of steam. Charlie lounged on the bed with her legs crossed, her hand rustling around a share bag of Doritos as she flicked through the TV guide. It all felt very... *domestic*. Normal.

Tamara cleared her throat and searched for her hairbrush, finding it on the dresser. "It was needed after all that drama," she replied, sitting in front of the vanity mirror and carefully combing through her thick, damp hair. She felt bare without her usual makeup, clad in a pink satin romper that didn't cover much of her cleavage or thighs. It had been a long time since she'd gotten ready for bed with somebody else. She'd cherished that solitude after the divorce until it had soured to loneliness, but she'd forgotten just how vulnerable sharing a routine with somebody could make her feel.

Charlie's reflection shifted in the mirror. She turned on her side to face Tamara, her head propped on her fist. "Bet you're

First Comes Marriage

regretting all this now, aren't you?"

Pausing, Tamara locked eyes with Charlie in the mirror. "I didn't think it would be easy. I just didn't think—"

"That you'd marry an impulsive idiot with anger issues and a shit tonne of baggage?"

She sighed, squeezing a dollop of lavender-scented hand cream into her palm and massaging it into her skin. She'd need all the help she could get with sleeping tonight. "We all have baggage. But no, I didn't exactly think I'd be married to Charlie Dean."

"I didn't think I'd be married to Tamara Hewitt," Charlie replied, a smile curling slowly across her face. It made Tamara want to smile back, brush her fingers along the dimples of her cheeks just to know what they felt like. What she felt like. She flushed at the thought, distracting herself by sorting through her skincare products. But she paused again when Charlie added, "I'm lucky. Being married to any of the others... no, thanks."

"Don't get too romantic," Tamara murmured, though the backhanded compliment felt like a compliment all the same. And she supposed Charlie was right. She couldn't imagine going through this with any of the other contestants. If nothing else, she and Charlie shared an understanding, and it was making things much easier than they had been at the altar. They were in this together.

Her fingers hovered over her favourite tissue face masks, eucalyptus and honey-scented. "You know what we need?" she asked, brandishing the shiny foil packets.

Charlie groaned. "Oh, no."

"Oh, yes." Grinning, Tamara threw one of the face masks to Charlie and kept another for herself. "Do we have cucumbers?"

Chapter Eleven

"I know you're a model and all that, but this is too much even for me. I'm not into girly shit."

"Right," she teased. "Super metal rock star Charlie Dean is way too cool for skin care. But you'll regret it when you look like a prune at forty. You won't be young and pretty forever, you know."

"A *prune?*" Charlie repeated, voice rising in disbelief.

"I haven't seen you drink one glass of water since we met. Your skin is begging to be hydrated."

Charlie rolled her eyes, and Tamara thought that would be the end of it — only, a moment later, she tore open the packet and grimaced. "Smells like shit."

"I'm going to find a cucumber. I can see a hint of crow's feet there." Tamara wiggled her finger by Charlie's eye as she passed, and Charlie slapped her hand away with a scowl.

"Cheeky sod."

Giggling, Tamara padded down the hallway to the kitchen before Charlie changed her mind. It was pristine as though never used before, just like the rest of the rustic-style cottage. If there weren't cameras hidden on every piece of furniture, she might have enjoyed the comfort of it all, even with Charlie and the chaos she brought.

Only basics were stocked in the fridge: ready meals, milk, butter. She sighed and boiled the kettle instead, plucking four tea bags from the pastel-green tin and placing them in a mug. Once the water boiled, she steeped the tea bags before draining them and squeezing out the excess water. She had no idea if tea bags were much use, but they'd make do. She just needed an excuse to sit back and not think for a moment, and this was how she relaxed at home.

She took the tea bags back into the bedroom to find Charlie

First Comes Marriage

still fiddling with her own mask, her upper lip curling in disgust as she wiped her hand on her black T-shirt. "It's all... *wet*."

"It's supposed to be. Put it on your face."

"What the fuck are those?" she asked, eyeing the plate of cooling tea bags.

"Couldn't find any cucumber," Tamara explained, sitting beside Charlie on the bed and opening her own mask. She peeled it out of the packet and smoothed it onto her face, the cool tissue soothing her tired skin. "See?" she said, making sure the flaps for her mouth and eyes were in line with her features. "Feels nice."

Charlie shuddered. "It looks like something from a horror movie." Still, she awkwardly put the face mask on.

Tamara couldn't help but laugh at the sight, the slits positioned wonkily so one of the eye holes was on the tip of Charlie's nose. "Here." She lined the mask up, tracing her finger carefully along Charlie's hairline to smooth the wrinkles from the tissue.

Charlie's throat bobbed, a thick, strange, electric silence sparking between them. They were so close. Tamara's breath turned uneven, and she sat back and surveyed her work before she could think too much about it. Think about how, in these short moments, it sometimes felt more real than anything she'd known before. Charlie never pretended. She never gave Tamara the answers she wanted to hear or turned on a different, brighter personality when they had company. She was just Charlie: blunt, unfazed, sarcastic, volatile.

Difficult to navigate. Easy to laugh with.

Tamara regained her composure, dangling the drained tea bags in front of Charlie's face. "Lie back."

Grumbling, Charlie did, crossing her hands over her stomach as she pressed her head into the thick eiderdown pillows.

Chapter Eleven

"Nobody will ever know about this."

"Never," Tamara agreed, though everybody would see it tomorrow, no doubt. She placed the tea bags over Charlie's eyes, smiling to herself while imagining the world's reaction to Charlie Dean practising self-care.

She lay beside Charlie, dropping the tea bags over her own eyes and shutting out the world. The TV played quietly, exhaustion settling into her bones and her mind scattering in a million different places. She took a few deep breaths as the residual anxiety of the busy day thrummed through her, not helped by the feeling of unfamiliarity, of not knowing what came next. But she was okay, she convinced herself.

A tingle crept along her finger as a pinkie brushed against hers. Charlie's. She locked them together, the rest of her as still as Tamara had ever seen. She was usually fidgeting or pacing. "You all right? I know it was a lot. The thing with Sloan... it's a lot," Charlie said, genuine compassion in her tone.

"I'm okay," Tamara promised. And then, because it was easier when she couldn't see anything, "Can I ask you a question?"

"Go on." Charlie's voice turned wary.

"Did you ever have feelings for Sloan?" Tamara wasn't sure she wanted to hear the answer, but she had to know. If there was something there, she had a right to know. Even if it seemed like Charlie hated her guts, people kept asking her and acting like she should be worried. Maybe it was getting to her a little bit.

And she couldn't help but wonder what it had taken to make Charlie betray her friend that way. Whether it had been worth it or just what Charlie had said: a drunken one-night stand. It was the thing that divided them, the thing that made Tamara feel worlds apart from Charlie. She'd never been good at

First Comes Marriage

casual. And despite believing that Charlie was sorry, that she felt terrible, she didn't know if she could trust her completely yet.

"No." Charlie's fingers clenched around Tamara's own. "I mean, she was attractive at the time, but no. She was just in the right place at the right time."

"Okay." There was so much more Tamara wanted to ask, but she didn't know how. She wasn't sure she even had a right to know.

"Not jealous, are you?" She could hear the smirk in Charlie's voice.

"No." Tamara shook her head, though Charlie couldn't see it, a spike of unease running through her.

"You wouldn't need to be, anyway. I was out of it that night. I barely even remember it. If it weren't for the pictures—"

"It's not like I'm worried you'll run off with her or something." Tamara laughed in an attempt to keep it light, but it lacked any mirth. "It's just that she's going to try to use it against us. It's pretty clear she's not forgotten, and it seems like maybe she wants to cause problems for us. It's better if we're in this together, and I just… I should know things. You know, just in case she tries to stir things up again."

"I've told you everything, Tamara," Charlie said. "She could have been anyone that night. I *wish* she would have been anyone else."

"Okay." Tamara squeezed her hand again. She had no reason not to believe her. She *wanted* to believe her.

"You know… you were right. I can't keep entertaining her, giving her what she wants. I just want to focus on getting through this shit so we can go back to normal life."

This shit. It shouldn't have stung, but it did. Tamara inched

Chapter Eleven

her hand away slowly, willing her throat to stop aching with the threat of tears. She'd forgotten for a moment that they were only here to clear their names. To get through the show and hopefully return to their very different careers at the end of it.

"Right. Of course." She sat up, catching the tea bags in her hands and putting them back on the plate before peeling off the mask. She massaged the excess serum into her skin carefully, trying to ignore Charlie's gaze as she pulled her own tea bags off to watch. "I'm exhausted. I think I'm going to call it a night. How are we...?" She eyed the bed. It was more than big enough for the two of them, but was still strange to share it like this. "I mean, are you okay with sleeping in the same bed? I think the couch is a pull-out—"

"We're adults, love." Charlie snatched her mask off inelegantly and crumpled it into a soggy ball, leaving it on the nightstand beside her. "I'm sure we can manage like this."

"Okay. Goodnight, then." Flicking the lamp off beside her, Tamara settled beneath the duvet with her back turned to Charlie. She didn't know why everything hurt all of a sudden. She wished it wouldn't.

She felt the mattress ripple beside her as Charlie got comfortable, their feet brushing just for a moment as she turned the television off and then her own lamp. "Night."

But Tamara didn't sleep for a long, long time, listening to Charlie's slowing breaths with fistfuls of the duvet in her hands. *Twelve more weeks,* she kept reminding herself. *It'll all be over in twelve weeks.*

It wasn't the comfort it had once been.

Chapter Twelve

A pparently, it was "First Dates Day". Charlie and Tamara had woken this morning to a note under the door announcing it as such, with the instruction to dress up nice and go to the dining room at six p.m. It had been signed by Sandra and contained within a sickening hand-drawn love heart. The upside was that they'd seen couples coming and going from the main house all day, and they hadn't had to interact with any of them, including Sloan. Charlie hoped it would stay that way.

They walked hand in hand to the main house that evening, the sky a lovely, mottled shade of British grey. Tamara had certainly followed Sandra's instructions in a velvet, burgundy dress with a ruched hem that left her golden, dimpled thigh on show. The material draped down to the base of her spine, a fact Charlie had only noticed as she led Tamara out of the door and grazed her fingers against Tamara's vertebrae. She'd grown a bit lost for words, wanting to tell Tamara how nice she looked, but *nice* didn't cover it.

Chapter Twelve

Charlie had settled on a mesh top with tailored, high-waisted trousers, clothes she'd stolen from her stylist after an awards show. And, fine, perhaps her gaze lingered on their reflection in the large windows of the main house for just a few seconds. They looked good together. Better than people from two completely different walks of life should have looked. Charlie almost lost her footing as they reached the door.

"Here we go, I suppose," Tamara said, trepidation widening her smoky, glitter-painted eyes. "I haven't been on a first date in a long time."

Charlie opened the door and motioned her in. "I don't think I've ever been on one."

"*Never?*" Tamara's lips parted in surprise, waiting for Charlie to take her hand again as they wandered towards the dining room. The main house was quiet save for the faint sound of piano and violin strings drifting through the hallway and the rolling cameras following their every move.

"Nope." Charlie shrugged it off. She'd never had time or energy to waste on dates, nor the desire. She didn't particularly like people, and she'd only ever seen toxic codependency in her friends' relationships. Either that, or they got all gooey and pathetic and were always late because apparently nothing mattered more than a snog. "I'm a first-date virgin."

"Not for long." Tamara grinned as they crossed the threshold. They paused there, taking it in. The large dinner table they'd all sat at together last night had been swapped for an intimate bistro table for two, a candle flickering in the centre. A server in a black bow tie stood by, motioning for them to sit.

The server gave Tamara a pink envelope before brandishing a champagne bottle from an ice bucket at a small bar. When given no objections, he poured.

First Comes Marriage

Charlie felt as though she was in a silent movie and wanted to cringe. "What's the envelope, then?"

Tamara slit it open with her long thumbnail, pulling out a glittery card. Her eyes scanned across it. "It's from Sandra. The Cupids have left questions for us to ask each other and…" she turned the card over and groaned, "tasks. Well, not tasks. Instructions. Like feed each other strawberries and dance with each other."

"We basically did that at the wedding. God, they better not give us that lavender cake again."

She laughed, dropping the card and sipping her champagne. The server disappeared, and Charlie frowned. "Aren't they supposed to take your order first?"

"Maybe they'll just give us a plate of spaghetti to share like in *Lady and the Tramp.*"

"I'm the lady, obviously."

Tamara nudged Charlie's leg under the table, feigning shock. "*Excuse* me? Are you calling me a tramp?"

A laugh bubbled from Charlie without warning. That kept happening recently. Maybe she'd have to go to the doctors when she was out of here. Or it might just have been indigestion.

"All right. We all know I'm the tramp. I mean, look at you." Charlie hadn't meant to let the words slip out. She clamped her lips down as though it would take them back, but it was too late. The words were there, hanging between them with the fairy lights. Her face burned, and she looked away quickly.

Thick silence settled between them, but not thick enough to smother the words away. Tamara twirled her champagne flute in her hand, eyes cast down. "Shall I start asking the questions, then?"

Charlie sighed and lay back in her seat, preparing herself. "Go

106

Chapter Twelve

on then."

It wasn't lost on her that this was where the good TV usually began. Maybe it was good she was giving compliments, even if it was accidental. It would make their relationship look more real, and that's what they'd agreed to, hadn't they? To make it look real. It was a lot less challenging than it had felt when Tamara had proposed the plan on the day of the wedding.

"Okay..." Tamara narrowed her eyes and shifted in her seat. "What's one thing you've always wanted to do but never had the guts to?"

Charlie didn't miss a beat before answering, "A fivesome."

A disbelieving choke exploded from Tamara mid-sip, and her champagne ended up spraying across the table on Charlie. Charlie closed her eyes, face dripping. "Nice."

"Sorry!" Tamara launched herself up, grabbing a napkin and dabbing an amused Charlie frantically. Her chin, her forehead, her nose. It was everywhere. Her face reddened and she grew flustered. Charlie felt like a five-year-old being wiped down by their mother after a chocolatey dessert. "Sorry, sorry, sorry."

Charlie's face scrunched but then she started laughing hysterically, a hand pressed to her chest. "I'm sorry. I couldn't help it."

That she was joking, teasing, seemed to dawn on Tamara too late, and sourly, she threw the damp, crumpled napkin at Charlie before sitting back down. "Ha, ha. Very funny."

"Oh, come on." Charlie wiped the last of the champagne from her cheek with a smirk. "It was a *bit* funny."

"You enjoy making people uncomfortable, don't you?"

"On the contrary, it comes quite naturally." Her face pinched with seriousness as she leaned onto the table, closer to Tamara. In a low, velvety voice, she asked, "Do I make you uncomfortable,

First Comes Marriage

Tamara?"

Charlie had forgotten about the cameras. She'd forgotten about everything but the deep throb in the very pits of her stomach and the goosebumps rising along her arm. Curiosity kept her suspended at the table.

Tamara licked her lips and blinked, sitting back stiffly. "You make me impatient. Irritated. Exhausted. Need I go on?"

Charlie rolled her eyes playfully but didn't move, didn't lengthen the distance between them, as a twinge of disappointment rolled through her. "That's no way to talk to your other half." She twirled the stem of her glass between her fingers. "A hot air balloon ride. That's one thing I've always wanted to do but never had the guts to. Happy now?"

"Afraid of heights?"

"Not so much heights as trusting a balloon and a basket to keep me from falling to my death. How about you?"

Clearing her throat, Tamara tucked her hair behind her ear bashfully. "Mine's a silly one. I've always wanted to dye my hair a bright colour. Everyone tells me I shouldn't because it'll ruin my natural colour, and, y'know, I'm paid to look nice."

Charlie scanned Tamara's face, her hair, for a moment. She couldn't imagine having a career built from appearance. Then again, her fame had grown superficial just as fast. Everyone had a say in how she looked. She spent hours doing photo shoots for magazines and album covers, no matter how much she rebelled.

"You'd suit pastels," she said.

Tamara smoothed down her waves. "You think?"

A nod. Charlie did think. She thought too much. About Tamara, about them, about the changes happening between them. "What's next then?" she asked in a desperate attempt to break the sudden tension.

Chapter Twelve

Tamara examined the questions again. "Let's see... What made you want to get married?"

Charlie held her hand up, the golden band glinting against the guttering candlelight. "The jewellery."

Tamara snorted, nudging her with her toe again. "Come on. Didn't you ever fantasise about being married growing up?"

Wrinkling her nose, Charlie shook her head. "I fantasised about being a rock star. Not washing someone else's dishes."

"There's more to marriage than that. Didn't you ever hope to have someone by your side? Someone who had your back no matter what? Someone who *chose* you?"

Her mouth dried up. She'd never imagined that, not really. She was too used to being alone. But it was clear that Tamara wanted it. Her eyes glittered hungrily, desperately.

A twinge of guilt ran through Charlie. "I never really thought about it that way. I was always a lone wolf growing up."

"So why now?"

She frowned. Tamara knew why now. She knew that Charlie hadn't had a choice. "Why not?" was all she could answer with.

Tamara's face flickered with disappointment, but Charlie couldn't understand why. What was she expecting?

She continued with the questions: "Do you ever want to have kids?"

Charlie shuddered dramatically. "Fuck, no... Do you?"

A shrug. "I don't feel like it would necessarily fulfill me the way it's supposed to. Like maybe I'm not maternal enough or something. I'd want to build the rest of my life first, hopefully with another person, and then we'll see."

"Interesting." Another way they weren't compatible. Or maybe another way they were. Charlie always felt like she'd been waiting for something more. She'd thought music and

First Comes Marriage

fame would bring it, but… there was still something missing. Maybe there always would be. Until she figured out a way to fill that hole, she wasn't sure she'd ever be ready for all the adult stuff. Relationships and kids.

"Tell me about your longest relationship," said Tamara.

Charlie huffed a long breath and braced her elbows on the table. It had been so long, she barely remembered. "I was eighteen, I think. We were together for four months, maybe? God, aren't there any more exciting questions on there?"

With a frown, Tamara opened her mouth, but whatever she was going to say was cut off by the server's return. He set down two covered silver platters and left them to it. "We have to guess each other's favourite food, it says."

Charlie looked at her own covered dish. She was absolutely certain she'd asked Jed to make up answers to the interview questions asked by the Cupids in the early stages of the show, too lazy and too pissed off to take them seriously. Jed had probably given her something she hated out of spite, like cottage pie or smelly stilton. She eyed Tamara's plate for a moment. "I'm going to guess yours is something fancy like beef Wellington."

Tamara tutted and lifted her cover to reveal… what looked to be sticky toffee pudding and custard. A much, much better answer than Charlie could have expected. "Beef Wellington?" Tamara repeated in disbelief. "You must think I'm so boring."

Charlie couldn't help but chuckle. "All right. I underestimated you."

"I think yours is something greasy like a burger. Oh!" Tamara snapped her fingers excitedly. "Nachos. You ordered nachos at the hotel the other day."

"Final answer?"

She nodded.

Chapter Twelve

"Okay…" Something fluttered in Charlie, because Tamara was right. She did love nachos. She'd claimed plenty of times that they would be her last meal, smothered in guacamole, sour cream, salsa, and a mountain of cheese. And Tamara had noticed. She'd paid attention.

With bated breath, Charlie lifted the lid. On the plate lay a loaded tray of nachos covered in all of the toppings she loved, including spring onions and crunchy bacon. *Thank you, Jed.*

"I was right!" Tamara bounced in her seat excitedly. "You have to share now. It's the rules."

Charlie smirked and pushed the plate to the centre of the table. Tamara did the same with her sticky toffee pudding, and if only to tease her, Charlie nabbed the spoon and licked away the custard and crumbs. She moaned in delight, the sugar and vanilla tingling on her tongue. "Yummy."

"No! No, those aren't the rules!" Tamara tried to snatch the spoon away, but Charlie was quicker, raising it in the air before she could reach.

"Sharing is caring!" Charlie sing-songed. Tamara's pout almost made her melt. Almost. She was a rock star, of course. She wasn't affected by pretty pouting women. Definitely not.

Vengeance flaring her nostrils, Tamara grabbed a nacho and loaded it with guacamole, downing it in one so the smashed avocado almost spilt out of her mouth. "I want a divorce."

Charlie couldn't help but grin, surrendering the dessert finally. "Promise?"

Somehow, though, a divorce was the last thing on her mind.

Chapter Thirteen

Settling into a strange new life with Charlie had become… okay, somehow, for Tamara. Things had been easier since that first date. They could laugh with each other now. Tamara became less aware of the cameras following them around the village, and even of Sloan's constant daggers whenever they were forced into the main house for dinners or silly tasks that would make for interesting TV.

It wasn't normal life, and Tamara knew that. She still felt slightly more laid bare than ever, especially on the days she didn't bother with much makeup, but they were having fun and slowly making friends with Rafi, Alessandro, and Shell, and it wasn't as isolating or forced as she'd dreaded. In fact, it was a little bit like being on holiday.

She lay awake on the fourteenth morning in the cottage, staring up at the ceiling as Charlie's gentle snores whistled rhythmically beside her. Another thing she'd gotten used to. Learned to like, even. It made her feel less alone when she woke up forgetting where she was. She'd been spending a lot of time

Chapter Thirteen

wondering what was happening beyond this little bubble they'd made, wondering if Nadine was back in London setting up shoots for Tamara, whether Tamara was coming across okay to the public or whether they hated her even more now her face was on their television screens every night. Wondering whether Dominic ever saw the show. Saw her happy with Charlie in a strange sort of way. Nothing had happened between them, but they held hands a lot. Charlie was more touchy-feely now, and sometimes they lay closer than they needed to in bed.

And then Tamara realised that she didn't particularly care what Dominic would think of that. She didn't care if he saw anything. He crept into her thoughts less and less these days, and she wanted it to stay that way.

"I can hear the cogs turning in your brain." Charlie's murmur, thick with sleep, startled Tamara.

She turned over with her head still on the pillow to face her, finding her eyes half-open and her cheek squished atop her hand. Her hair was mussed, sticking up at all ends endearingly, and a trickle of warmth spread through Tamara at the sight. She liked waking up next to Charlie. It made her feel special. No one else in the world had that privilege now. Only she got to see Charlie out of the spotlights and the tabloids.

Tamara only hummed, giving a small good morning smile.

"What are you thinking about?" Charlie asked.

"Just what things will be like when we leave. It's weird, having no access to the outside world. We could have a new prime minister and we wouldn't even know."

Charlie wrinkled her nose. "God, I hope so." Sidling slightly closer, she traced her finger along Tamara's bare arm, and Tamara fought a shudder. "Honestly, I thought I'd hate all this. I'm usually the first person to pack up and go when I get bored.

First Comes Marriage

I don't like keeping still for too long."

"Is there a reason for that?" Tamara questioned softly.

Charlie shrugged. "You get used to it with all the touring. But I suppose I've just never had a reason to stick around anywhere for too long. I like keeping busy."

"So are you saying you're planning on doing a runner?" Tamara was only half-joking. She'd almost forgotten who Charlie was. How different they were in the real world.

"I'm saying the opposite." Charlie poked Tamara's rib lightly. "It's nice. My head feels... quiet, for the first time in a long time."

An overwhelming wave of something foreign washed over Tamara at the confession. Something that made her feel warm and peaceful and glad. "Me too," she admitted quietly, adjusting her head on the pillow. It left their noses only inches away from brushing, so close that the watery morning light and sheer curtains were just a blur behind Charlie. She was the only thing in focus.

Tamara glanced at the wedding ring on her finger, thinking again of what came next. She couldn't imagine taking it off now. But there would be a life after this. A life where she woke up alone in the mornings again. Wouldn't there?

The future felt fuzzy when Tamara thought of it. She didn't know. She couldn't see rock star Charlie Dean sticking around once the cameras were off. But this Charlie, sleep-softened and serene....

Charlie leaned closer, their noses grazing, and Tamara stopped breathing. "Tam—"

An almighty wail sliced through whatever Charlie had wanted to say, startling them until they broke apart. Confusion creased Charlie's tired features as she snapped up. "What the fuck is that?"

Chapter Thirteen

"It sounds…" Tamara gulped, her eyes falling to the closed bedroom door as the high-pitched noise broke into three sharp inhales of breath and then started all over again. "It sounds like a baby."

"Oh, fuck no!" Charlie was up in a flash, wearing only her briefs and a ratty, oversized Joy Division T-shirt. Tamara tried not to stare at her long, tattooed legs, instead climbing out of bed and shucking on her silk robe.

By the time she'd knotted the belt around her waist, Charlie's voice bellowed from downstairs: "Oh, *fuck* no!"

That didn't sound promising. Tamara stumbled down the narrow stairwell, the wails getting louder the closer she came to the sitting room. She soon found out why. There, where Charlie stood hunched and gaping, a pale yellow cot had miraculously replaced their coffee table. Inside it was a baby. A plastic one, mind, but still. A crying baby.

Tamara almost dropped a few expletives herself. Biting her lip, she wandered over to the cot, wincing against the shrieks as she picked up a pink envelope labelled with their names. Inside was a handwritten letter from the Cupids:

"Dear Charlie and Tamara," she read aloud, *"this week's task as newlyweds is to prepare for family life. You must dive into parenthood and make sure to keep your new bundle of joy fed, clothed, and cared for. At the end of the week, the couple with the happiest baby will win a special date!"*

"Nope." Charlie rubbed her eyes dramatically, turning her back to the screaming infant. "I don't give a fuck about going on a date. I'm not doing this."

Tamara couldn't help but smirk, placing the letter on the couch and reaching into the cot for the lifelike doll. "Oh, come on," she chided, picking it up and rocking it gently, "it'll be fun."

First Comes Marriage

"Your definition of fun is worrying."

"But look at her!" Tamara shoved the doll in Charlie's face, earning a comical flinch from Charlie. "She's so cute!" Assuming it was a *she*, anyway, being as it wore a pink hat. Outdated idea of gender, she knew, but she *felt* like a girl.

"Didn't you ever watch *Chucky*?"

"Oh, don't listen to her, little baby," cooed Tamara and the cries eased as she did, causing her to rock the baby more enthusiastically. "You're cute, aren't you? What shall we name you?"

"I feel like I'm on drugs," Charlie deadpanned, collapsing onto the couch with a huff.

"We should call her... Lavender!" Tamara suggested. "Because that's the cake we had for our wedding."

Charlie shook her head as though at the end of her tether, which only made Tamara want to tease her more. "We're not naming our baby after a bloody cake that didn't even taste nice."

"Fine. What about Marina? The name of the beach where we got married?" The baby let out a pleasant burble at that. "Oh, yes. That's your name, isn't it?"

Muttering under her breath, Charlie lay back and propped her bare feet on the couch, rubbing her temples. "I'm in hell."

"You're so dramatic." Tamara tutted and placed Marina on Charlie's chest. "You hold her while I have a look through this bag." The large, pale, pink shoulder bag had been placed on the floor next to the cot. Tamara could admit that, when she opened it, she felt a little bit overwhelmed. Nappies, wet wipes, fake baby food and empty bottles, clothes, and dummies filled the bag, as well as rattles and stuffed toys. If the baby wasn't made of plastic and rubber, she might have run out of the door herself.

Chapter Thirteen

The cries returned almost immediately after. "Nope," Charlie said again, holding Marina above her head as though she was a rugby ball about to be thrown. "Take her back. She doesn't like me."

Tamara rolled her eyes and took Marina again, rocking her side to side. This time, it did nothing to soothe her. "I think she needs feeding. Will you get the milk bottles out of the bag?"

"I'm going for a shower," Charlie muttered, already strutting away.

"Charlie!" Tamara shouted after her, but it was too late. Charlie was gone.

And Tamara, apparently, was a single mother.

* * *

Charlie was quite sure she was in hell. She walked into a room of crying babies and tired celebrities after being forced to spend the rest of the day co-parenting in the main house. And if that wasn't enough, she'd just suffered through another visit to Cupid's Conservatory, where Sandra grilled the contestants on their marriages so far. She plonked down on the couch beside Rafi, sure to avoid direct eye contact with Sloan. She'd been treating her like Medusa these past two weeks, and so far, it had worked.

Tamara was in the kitchen helping with lunch, and Charlie hated to admit that she didn't know what to do with herself when she was left alone with the others. As though sensing it, Rafi stopped burping his baby and gave her a smile. "How are things going with you and Tamara? You seem close."

"Yeah, I suppose we are." Heat prickled in Charlie's face inexplicably, and she propped her ankle on her knee awkwardly.

First Comes Marriage

"You really like her then?" he pried.

She shrugged. "I do." Not a lie, either. Tamara had certainly grown on her, to the point where Charlie kept having to remind herself that it wasn't real; that she couldn't just kiss Tamara when she wanted to, which was often, or wrap her arms around her waist when they were alone. "What about you and Alessandro?"

"He's... hard to read," Rafi admitted, propping his soothed baby on a cushion beside him. "I don't know if he likes me or not. He just talks about onions a lot."

Charlie couldn't help but snort, though she had noticed that Alessandro was very passionate about his food. An Italian Gordon Ramsay, she'd labelled him when they'd gone round to their cottage for dinner a few nights ago and he'd thrown a tantrum about the quality of Tamara's hors d'oeuvres. "Do you like him?"

"I want it to work," Rafi said. "I think I'm just waiting for a sign that it's right. How did you know with Tamara?"

She paused, the question taking her aback. All right, she and Tamara were getting on surprisingly well, but she wasn't a bloody love guru. Charlie Dean did not offer relationship advice. Then again, Charlie Dean didn't usually entertain relationships at all, and now she had a baby—

Oh, shit. Where is Marina? Why had she not been tortured by the crying baby in over five minutes? Charlie had left her bundled in blankets in her Moses basket beside the couch. She straightened up, peering over the arm and wincing. Not there. "Has Tam been in here?"

"No, I don't think so."

She must have been, Charlie convinced herself. The baby could hardly have gone on a walkabout on her own. *Unless she*

Chapter Thirteen

is Chucky.

"I'm just going to…." She didn't bother to finish her sentence, wandering into the large, modern kitchen where Alessandro was concocting God knows what. Tamara stood by the hob with one hand on her hip, stirring a bubbling pot of spaghetti. No Marina in sight.

"Tam…?"

Tamara whipped her head up, cheeks rosy from the hot steam. "Yep?"

"Where's the baby?"

She frowned, abandoning the spoon in the pot. "You had her."

"Yeah, but then I was called into the conservatory so I left her in that basket thing." It felt ridiculous even calling a doll "her" but she'd already been shouted at for naming Marina "it" once this morning. Tamara had grown very attached.

"You left her on her own?"

"Only for…" she looked at the clock and realised it had been much longer—Sandra certainly loved to talk—"half an hour," she finished gingerly.

Tamara clamped her lips in annoyance, yanking off her personalised apron and leaving it on the counter. "Where did you leave her?"

"In the sitting room by the couch."

"Maybe someone else took her by mistake." She led Charlie back into the bustling sitting room, and together they scanned each baby. Shell was reading *The Miracle of Mindfulness* to her baby, and Jack was playing catch with his. Rafi still sat on the couch, now feeding his baby, and….

Charlie narrowed her eyes as she caught Sloan's gaze. She was painting her nails a crimson red while her baby cried beside her. No sign of Marina, but if there were any kidnappers in the

First Comes Marriage

room, Charlie had an idea of who it might have been.

Without thinking, she marched up to Sloan and crossed her arms. "Have you resorted to child abduction now?"

"Pardon?" Sloan smirked, looking up at Charlie from under thick black lashes.

"Have you stolen the fucking doll?" Charlie spat out.

Feigning innocence, Sloan shook her head with wide eyes. "Why would I do that?"

Charlie felt Tamara's presence at her back, and a moment later, her hand around Charlie's wrist. Tamara tugged her away. "Let's just have another look for her."

"Motherhood suits you, Charlie." Sloan's drawl followed her out of the sitting room, but Charlie didn't have the energy to make a retort. If she'd honestly taken their pretend baby, Charlie had no interest in causing a scene. It was pathetic.

It made her wonder if it had been Sloan who let Ali into the hotel room that day. It seemed as though she enjoyed playing games and being in the public eye. Charlie wouldn't keep adding fuel to her fire.

"That was very… calm of you," Tamara remarked as they went back into the kitchen. Charlie started searching the cupboards, much to the annoyance of Alessandro, who was frantically trying to manage three pots and pans at once.

"I can't be arsed with her anymore," Charlie admitted, for the first time wondering why. Perhaps because it had been so much easier, better, to manage these last two weeks without rising to Sloan. Perhaps because she'd found something in the cottage she'd never known before. Removed from the drama and expectations of everyday life, with only Tamara for company…. It was nice. It felt untouchable, the one thing in her life that nobody, not even herself, could ruin.

Chapter Thirteen

"Good. I'm glad I don't have to pull you away from another fight." Tamara shot her a soft smile before searching the fridge. As soon as the door was opened, a baby toppled out and fell onto the kitchen tiles. Marina.

Her crying rent through the entire house as Tamara picked her up, cradling her into her shoulder and patting her back. "Did that mean lady put you in the fridge?"

Despite her hatred for both real and pretend babies, Charlie sighed in relief.

"Oh good. You found her," a familiar voice crooned behind them.

Charlie whipped around, finding Sloan standing with a satisfied grin on her face. Enough was enough. Charlie clenched her jaw and asked, "Can I have a word, Sloan?"

"You can have more than that, babe."

Tamara cast Charlie a wary glance. Ignoring the double meaning, Charlie marched out of the kitchen, through the sitting room, and into the empty library. Sloan followed, draping herself across the leather loveseat and waiting expectantly.

"What are you doing, Sloan?" Charlie asked finally. Her voice thickened with unexpected emotion, stomach swirling. She was so tired of this. So tired of the guilt and the regret. So tired of pretending nothing touched her.

"I don't know what you mean."

"Yes, you do, and I've had enough. I'm trying to move on."

Sloan scoffed. "With Tamara Hewitt?"

She said her name with so much venom that Charlie's hands balled into fists. But she remained still. Calm.

"Maybe, yeah. It doesn't matter who or how. I'm trying to move on, and you're trying to play games, and I'm bored of it. I'm not here for you. We had one night together. One stupid

First Comes Marriage

night. I was so wasted I can barely remember it. So why are you doing this? Why can't you just let it lie?"

Sloan pursed her lips together, for once speechless. She crossed her legs, looking anywhere but at Charlie.

"Is it just for the cameras or something?" Charlie continued. "If it is, there are a dozen people here who want to be reality stars. Mess around with them instead. I'm not interested. I'm trying to move on from my mistakes."

"Right," Sloan snorted, "that's why you came on this show. To move on from your mistakes and play happy family with some model. Please, Charlie. Everyone knows you too well to believe you're here for anything but the fame. It's embarrassing, all this pretending. Does Tamara even know how fake it is?"

"Tamara knows a hell of a lot more than you," Charlie replied quietly, fixing her gaze on Sloan. "I won't ask you again. I'm not interested in doing this with you anymore. Please, just stop."

She hated to beg. Hated to show any hint of weakness. But it had gone on long enough. She couldn't stop thinking about what Yasmin must have thought if she watched their interactions. How much it would hurt to have their history rehashed over and over. Charlie didn't want to be that person anymore. She wanted to be whoever she was now, wanted to spend her evenings letting Tamara do her makeup or watch documentaries together. Funny how her life felt more real now, under constant scrutiny, than it had before the show. Funny how she'd spent years perfecting a fucked-up, messy, reckless facade for the sake of "rock 'n' roll" only to come in here and have it torn away by someone she'd once thought more artificial than her.

"Oh my god," Sloan said, "are you serious? You really like her that much?"

122

Chapter Thirteen

"It's not just about her," Charlie answered, fiddling with the belt loop on her jeans. "I lost everything after what we did. I'm trying to put my life back together, and coming here has made me *want* to. Whatever you're trying to do, however you're trying to come across… just keep me out of it."

Sloan raised a sharp brow, weighing Charlie up for a moment. Charlie was certain she caught a glitter of something real in her eye. "All right. Fine."

Charlie nodded, making to leave, but she stopped at the doorway and turned back. "That morning after…Was it you who let Ali French into the hotel?"

"I don't know what you mean." Sloan jutted her chin into the air, but something in her composure wobbled. Was that regret behind the smirk?

It was gone too fast for Charlie to make it out. Either way, it was over now. Charlie couldn't control how Sloan acted, but she could control her own life, her own reactions. She could try to be better than the person she had been a year ago.

So she left the library, left Sloan, left that awful night behind, and returned to the sitting room, to Tamara.

* * *

Tamara soon found out that Marina slept very little. That night, she grumbled as she was woken again by the baby's cries, prodding Charlie on the back until she stirred beside her in the darkness. "Your turn."

"No," Charlie groused.

"Your turn." Tamara continued poking her, moving up and down her shoulders until she finally sighed.

"Who the fuck would choose to be a parent?" she murmured,

First Comes Marriage

standing up.

Tamara nestled further into the pillows, making the most of both sides of the bed. Still, minutes passed and Marina continued to wail over Charlie's occasional curses. "Have you burped her?" she shouted, rubbing her eyes. It was clear she wouldn't get any more sleep for a while.

"I'm telling you this thing is cursed!" Charlie replied. "Either that or it's broken from being in the fridge."

"Or traumatised," Tamara murmured. She hauled herself out of bed, her entire body sluggish after a day spent mothering a doll. When she trudged downstairs, she found Charlie holding Marina... upside down. "No wonder she's bloody crying! She's the wrong way up!"

"I'm trying to reset it." Charlie's eyes narrowed in the dim light as she peeled off the striped bodysuit and the nappy beneath, searching.

Protectively, Tamara snatched Marina away and began rocking her, shifting from foot to foot. Perhaps she had gotten a little bit attached to the doll, but she wasn't the only one. Jack had asked earlier if he could breastfeed his baby, leading to a lesson in sex education taught by Ella and Dane. It wasn't that she wanted kids anytime soon. She just liked pretending with Charlie sometimes. Liked having something to focus on other than the growing butterflies in her gut. This reminded her that it was just a game, an act, a show. Not real.

"Did you feed her?" she asked.

Charlie rolled her eyes. "If by *feed*, you mean put an empty milk bottle in her plastic lips, then yes. Isn't this a bit ridiculous now? We've already lost. She spent half an hour crying in a fridge this afternoon."

"I'm beginning to think you don't love our child," Tamara

Chapter Thirteen

teased, though she supposed Charlie was right. Sloan had made sure they wouldn't win the special date at the end of the week. "We still have four days. We have to join in."

"But at…" Charlie checked the clock hanging on the wall, "two a.m.?"

"Oh, don't give me that. I bet you were out partying at two a.m. before all this."

"Yes, but there are no screaming children in clubs. They're forbidden, in fact."

Marina began to calm, nestled into Tamara's chest. Yawning, Tamara sank down into the armchair and continued drawing soothing circles into her back. It was the only thing that seemed to work, which made no sense, being as she surely couldn't have felt it. Charlie sprawled out on the couch just like she had that morning, watching them quietly.

"What?" Tamara's cheeks heated. She couldn't help but think about this morning. They'd been so close. She'd been sure Charlie was going to kiss her. But it hadn't been mentioned since, and they were probably better off that way.

"You said you weren't maternal." Charlie's voice was soft. Different. *Probably just tiredness*, Tamara tried to brush off.

She shrugged. "I don't *feel* maternal. If this was a real baby, I'd have no idea what to do." Silence passed between them, the ticking clock counting each second. "Nadine has a little niece. She just turned two. I suppose that's where it comes from. Kids are great as long as you can give them back."

"Words to live by." Charlie's feet dangled off the edge of the couch. She smiled, the moonlight leaving a stripe across her oversized shirt.

Marina burbled, and Tamara tucked her chin to her chest to look down at her. A moment later, a light snore droned from

125

First Comes Marriage

the doll. Still, she didn't move. She found herself wanting to savour every quiet moment with Charlie she could get.

"How did things go with Sloan?" She'd been wanting to ask all day, but part of her hadn't wanted to know. They'd both returned seeming quiet, Sloan retreating into the kitchen and barely showing her face for the rest of the day. Tamara would be lying if she'd said she hadn't felt a pang of something sharp and unpleasant. Charlie might have reassured her that she had no feelings for Sloan, but it was still odd, and Tamara's mind wandered nonetheless, just as it used to whenever Dominic came home late or was photographed with other women. It would always be there, that insecurity. Problem was, she had no reason to have it with Charlie. Charlie wasn't *hers*.

"I told her very politely to bugger off," Charlie replied with a sigh. "I'm tired of being this person, Tam. Everyone else is tired of it, too, and I don't blame them. Sloan brought out the worst parts of me, but I won't keep letting her have that power. I can't."

Tamara couldn't help but raise her brows. She had no idea what had brought on the change, but warmth swelled in her all the same. Maybe Charlie could finally see the good parts in herself; the parts that Tamara had been allowed to see since the plane journey home, when Charlie was there to take care of her.

Carefully, she stood and placed Marina in her cot before padding over to Charlie. Charlie lifted her legs, giving her space to sit on the opposite side before resting them on Tamara's thighs. They looked at one another for a moment that felt like a lifetime, Charlie's eyes piercing and bottomless. "I'm proud of you for deciding that. I half-expected I'd have to haul you out of a fight kicking and screaming."

Chapter Thirteen

"It crossed my mind." The corner of her mouth sunk with a smirk. "You were right. She isn't worth it. I've wasted so much time on things that just aren't worth it."

"Yeah." Tamara thought of Dominic. All the forgiveness she gave him, the time, the energy. The hope. That had been the worst part: hoping that if she just tried enough, eventually, he'd stop hurting her and they could be happy. "I know that feeling."

Charlie poked Tamara's torso with her big toe. "Am I included in that?"

It hadn't even crossed Tamara's mind that this might be a waste of time. She hoped she'd never see it that way. That, even after the show ended, she'd have these memories, this closeness, to look back on. Maybe even have Charlie in her life, somehow. "No. I thought this would be terrible, but... I like it. I like being around you. We have fun, don't we? This thing isn't so bad?"

Tamara's heart stuttered as she waited for the answer.

"No," Charlie said softly, "it isn't bad at all."

Tamara offered her a smile and then rested her head back, fatigue getting the better of her. Charlie didn't move, and neither did she. Not until she fell asleep, waking hours later to Marina's cries once again. They stayed on the couch together all night.

Chapter Fourteen

Sloan had left the village. They woke up on Friday morning to the news that she'd decided to quit the show, and Ella had left with her the previous evening. Charlie couldn't even pretend she wasn't relieved. Crying infants aside, the main house was much quieter as they gathered around the sitting room to find out who had won the challenge.

"Alessandro and Rafi," Shell announced, reading from another set of Cupid's cards, "after keeping your baby happiest and most cared for all week, you have won the challenge and will get to go on a glam picnic for two this evening." Shell bit her lip and grimaced in Charlie and Tamara's direction. "Charlie and Tamara, since you ended the week with the unhappiest baby, you have been chosen to prepare Alessandro and Rafi's date and wait on them all evening."

Charlie groaned into Tamara's shoulder dramatically. "It wasn't our fault our baby ended up in the fridge."

"Well… you are supposed to watch babies at all times," Dane reasoned. Charlie chose to ignore him, glimpsing Rafi's smug

Chapter Fourteen

smirk.

"I'm going to enjoy this," he said.

Charlie knew she absolutely wouldn't.

* * *

"This isn't so bad," Tamara said as she returned to the kitchen with a tray of dirty plates. Rafi and Alessandro were cuddled together on a picnic blanket outside, watching *Notting Hill* on a giant projector screen while the sun set over the tree-dotted hills. Of course, she'd rather be the one enjoying the romcom, but Rafi had gone easy on them. In the end. That's not to say he didn't enjoy messing with Charlie, asking her to wash every single grape and slice the cheeses into five-millimetre chunks.

She scowled, her hands covered in suds as she threw the last plates into the sink. "It's shit."

"Is it, though?" Proudly, Tamara brandished her gift: a champagne bottle she'd pilfered from Rafi and Alessandro's ice bucket on her way back into the house.

Charlie's eyes gleamed, cheeks cracking with a wide smile. "Oh, you beautiful woman, you. Did you steal it?" She examined the bottle, wasting no time in peeling back the foil.

"If I told you that, I'd have to kill you," Tamara feigned nonchalance, though her heart skipped at the unexpected compliment all the same.

Still grinning, Charlie deftly twisted the cork. With a pop, the champagne began to foam. Tamara nabbed two flutes from the cupboard, watching as Charlie expertly poured a healthy amount of champagne into each.

"Cheers," Tamara said, raising her flute as Charlie placed the bottle down and grabbed her own.

First Comes Marriage

"You're supposed to meet eyes when you say that, you know. Otherwise it's bad luck." She lifted her own drink, their glasses clinking, and this time, Tamara's gaze locked onto hers. "Cheers," Charlie murmured, smile falling just slightly, replaced by an intensity Tamara hadn't prepared for.

Neither of them made to drink. Tamara licked her lips, pulse throbbing through her. She'd been feeling like this more and more around Charlie. She didn't want to. It terrified her, especially when she knew there were a dozen cameras in this room alone. How much of their connection was real?

"Cheers," she whispered finally, downing her drink in one. She grabbed the freshly washed strawberries leftover in the bowl on the counter opposite, offering them out. "I saved us some."

"Thanks." Charlie plucked one from the bowl, teeth scraping across the seeds and lips reddening from the juice. Tamara drew her attention away quickly, biting into her strawberry and leaving the leaves on one of the dirty plates. The flavour burst across her tongue, sweetened by the champagne.

She pretended to be interested in the film outside. "This is one of my favourites."

"Oh, fuck no," Charlie protested. "I can't be married to a woman who enjoys *rom-coms*."

"I've been putting up with alien documentaries for weeks! You can pretend to enjoy a feel-good movie for once."

"No."

"For me?" Tamara pouted, nudging Charlie lightly.

Charlie smirked, shaking her head as her eyes returned to the screen. "I'll think about it. Hugh Grant is punching well above his weight, anyway. Why is Julia the one grovelling?"

They were at the infamous scene where Julia Roberts chases

Chapter Fourteen

Hugh Grant down and asks him to love her. It made Tamara cry every time. She could admit she craved grand gestures like that. She wanted a happily ever after. And, fine, she wanted Julia Roberts, but mostly she just wanted an epic love. A healthy one. One that made her heart sing.

Tamara mouthed the famous monologue with Julia, feeling the words resonate in her bones. Maybe she was tired of asking people to love her. Maybe that was the problem.

"Oh, bloody hell," Charlie said dryly, finishing off the last of her champagne and then topping off both flutes. "You really are a romantic, aren't you?"

"You have to be, don't you? What else is there to believe in anymore?"

"Alcohol," Charlie answered. "Music. Really good sex."

Tamara rolled her eyes and tried not to imagine that last part. She hadn't had really good sex in a very long time. She supposed she could do with that, too.

"It's sweet," Charlie continued, her fingers dancing across Tamara's carefully. "*You're* sweet."

"Oh, good. That's what every woman wants to hear, isn't it?" Tamara wrinkled her nose, a little bit breathless from Charlie's touch. "I'm sweet. Like a toddler. Or a cow."

"I didn't call you a cow!"

"The implication was there."

"You could just take the compliment," Charlie said, raising an eyebrow. They were close now, hips touching. The warmth of Charlie seeped through Tamara's clothes, her skin.

Tamara couldn't think of a comeback. Couldn't think of anything anymore. The champagne was making her dizzy, or maybe it was just Charlie. Charlie leaned forward, her eyes falling to Tamara's lips.

First Comes Marriage

"Can I?" Charlie asked.

Tamara feigned innocence. She wanted to hear Charlie say it. "Can you what?"

"Kiss you." It was whispered, barely audible, but it made Tamara's knees weak all the same. "I want to kiss you. I've wanted to..." Charlie trailed off as though there was no end to the sentence good enough.

So Tamara nodded weakly, holding her breath as Charlie's lips found hers. She could taste the champagne, the strawberries. It was enough to bring back the rest of her senses. Bring back the reminder that cameras were watching. A nation was watching. She didn't want this kiss to be for anyone but the two of them.

She pulled away quickly, a hand raised to Charlie's chest to keep her at arm's length.

Charlie's brows furrowed. "What's wrong?"

Tamara didn't have the words. She hadn't felt this vulnerable in a long, long time, but she refused to show it now. She refused to let it be televised, let this moment belong to the viewers too. She couldn't.

She staggered back and left the kitchen, ignoring Charlie's calls behind her as she trampled across the grass towards their cottage. The worst part about all of it was the doubt blooming in her chest. Because Charlie came here for her reputation. To play the happily married wife ready to settle down. And she was doing a stand-up job now, wasn't she?

If it is an act... if none of it is real....

The cracks began to burrow in Tamara's chest, a preview of the pain she'd feel if Charlie was just pretending to want her. She couldn't think with all the cameras. She couldn't *breathe*.

So she just kept running.

132

Chapter Fourteen

* * *

Charlie didn't know what had just happened. Tamara *wanted* to kiss her; she was sure of it. But then she disappeared.

Panicked, Charlie burst into the cottage only to be greeted with silence. It might have been a reprieve to finally be rid of the wailing baby if not for the fact that she needed to know what was happening. She needed Tamara.

She sprinted up the steps two at a time, finding the bathroom door locked. Of course. The one place without cameras.

Charlie gulped, pressing her head to the door for a moment to regain her breath. "Tam? Are you in there?"

No reply, but she heard the shuffling all the same.

"I just want to talk. I don't understand what just happened. Can you let me in, please?"

"Can you just give me a minute?" Tamara's voice was shaky behind the door, leaving Charlie's gut to wrench. Did she not want this? Did she already regret letting Charlie kiss her?

She'd thought that the feelings were mutual. That Tamara wanted her. It had been brewing between them for days, weeks, that chemistry. Charlie had never had anything like it before, with anyone. She'd never let anybody have the chance. But she'd chosen Tamara. She'd chosen to give in to it.

And it had only earned her a door slammed in her face.

"At least tell me you're okay," she begged.

"I'm fine, Charlie. Honestly." Tamara's words cracked with the lie, and Charlie fought the urge to roll her eyes. *Liar.*

"We need to talk about this. I need to know what's going on. Please." God, Charlie didn't do begging. She couldn't even remember the last time she'd said *please*. And now look at her. Weak and pathetic and uneasy because she couldn't see Tamara.

First Comes Marriage

Because she had no idea what was going on in her head.

A sigh gusted through the door. A moment later, the lock clicked and the door opened. Tamara's eyes were bloodshot, and the sight filled Charlie with dread as sharp and serrated as a knife.

"I'm fine," Tamara repeated, "just… overwhelmed."

"Because I kissed you?" Charlie asked.

Tamara nodded weakly. "Maybe. Yeah."

Charlie tugged the mic pack from her waistband and left it on the floor, abandoned. She wasn't willing to share something so personal with the world. This was about them. About Tamara.

Tamara eyed the pack warily and then stepped back as Charlie stepped forward, letting her into the bathroom. She moved her own mic and tossed it beside Charlie's, shirt riding up to reveal soft, beautiful stomach rolls. Charlie closed the door behind them, waiting expectantly.

"Did you not want to?" she asked quietly. She didn't know what she'd do if the answer was *no*. If all of this had been one-sided. Then again, she supposed it would be karma for all the shit she'd done to other women. The first time she'd felt something that went well beyond a quick fling, a drunken hook-up, and it was unrequited. She supposed she had that coming.

Tamara crossed her arms. "Want to what?"

"Kiss me?"

She closed her eyes and perched on the closed toilet seat. "I did. That's the problem."

Charlie's brows furrowed, heart beating so loud she was certain Tamara could hear it. "Why's that a problem?"

"Because… I'm getting confused." Throat bobbing, Tamara massaged her temples. "I can't tell what's real in here. We said we'd go along with this for the sake of our reputations, and now

Chapter Fourteen

I don't know... I don't know what's for the cameras and what's just you and me. I wanted that kiss to be just you and me."

"It was." Charlie's own throat felt hoarse as she knelt in front of Tamara, taking her hand. She hadn't even thought of the cameras when she'd asked to kiss Tamara. She'd forgotten all about them. If she hadn't, she might not have done it at all. She didn't need the whole nation to watch her turn gooey and desperate for someone. It was the last thing she wanted. It was the reason she'd spent so many years pretending she was just some one-dimensional musician, nothing more to her beyond sex, drugs, and rock 'n' roll. "It was just us, Tam. I didn't do it for the cameras or the show or my bloody reputation. That's well and truly ruined now anyway. I did it because I wanted to."

"Really?" Tamara lifted her gaze, eyelashes damp.

"Really." Charlie knew as she said it that it was true. She wanted Tamara. She wanted to kiss her until her lips were raw. She wanted to explore all the curves that had been teasing her for weeks. She wanted to tug more laughs from her. She wanted to listen to her singing in the shower every morning. There was no more hiding from it.

Tamara nudged herself forward, her hands crawling to the nape of Charlie's neck and leaving a shiver to travel down her spine. She'd never felt this sensitive, this needy. To prove it, she kissed Tamara slowly, deeply, softly, and roughly, her hand cupping Tamara's jaw. She was the sweetest thing Charlie had ever tasted, exactly as she'd imagined all those nights they'd lain in bed together. Gently, Charlie clamped her teeth down on Tamara's bottom lip, and she let out a breathy gasp, fingers knotting in Charlie's short hair.

"It shouldn't be this weird, kissing your own wife," Tamara said, a small giggle leaving her.

First Comes Marriage

Charlie chuckled too, nose lingering by Tamara's as she rested her hands on Tamara's soft, warm, round thighs. *It shouldn't be this good*, Charlie wanted to say, but she couldn't bring herself to. She stood up instead, holding out her hand for Tamara to take.

"Come on. I might let you watch a rom-com."

"*Let* me?" Tamara repeated with a scoff. Still, her cheeks dimpled as they wandered back to the bedroom together, leaving their microphones off and their doors shut. It was the best part of Charlie's day, slipping into bed with Tamara.

Even better now that she was allowed to kiss her.

Chapter Fifteen

The week before the first vote-out, Charlie found a box of pastel hair dyes in their kitchen. She frowned, placing the empty coffee mugs from the night before aside before examining them. A note from the Cupids had been laid out beside the dyes:

Good morning, newlyweds!

Today's challenge is all about creating new experiences with your partner while fulfilling your own goals. Tamara, on your first date with Charlie, you claimed that you've always wanted to dye your hair a bright colour — now's your chance!

Love,

The Cupids

Charlie couldn't stop the grin rising on her face. Tamara *had* said she'd always wanted to dye her hair.

As though summoned, Tamara trudged into the kitchen mid-yawn, her hair falling out of its ponytail and her pyjamas askew. Charlie had quickly learned that she was a restless sleeper, tossing and turning for most of the night and usually kicking

First Comes Marriage

Charlie in the process. "What should we have for breakfast?"

Without answering, Charlie picked up the hair dye and wiggled the box around excitedly. "Look what the Cupids left us this morning."

Frowning, Tamara examined the box. "Hair dye? Why?"

"For you." Charlie handed her the letter, and Tamara read it quickly.

"Oh, no. Oh God, no! I'm not dying my hair today."

"Oh, come on," Charlie urged, poking her in the ribs gently. "You said you always wanted to."

"Yeah, but there's no hairdresser in here in case it goes wrong. And then what? I'm on national telly with a funky hairdo and I'll probably never be hired again."

"I've used box dye plenty of times. I won't let it go wrong." She jutted her bottom lip out, pleading. Perhaps a part of her was sad that Tamara had always held back on these things for her job. Where Charlie was encouraged to be as eccentric as possible, Tamara faced the opposite. It made her wonder if perhaps modelling wasn't as easy as she'd thought. "Please?"

Tamara sighed. "Why isn't there anything in here for you?"

"Well, a fivesome would be a bit too saucy for prime-time TV, and a hot air balloon…." Charlie peered out the window just to be sure there were no hot air balloons waiting for her. Thankfully, she saw nothing but cottages and grass. "Probably not in the budget."

"Convenient," Tamara deadpanned.

"You're telling me there's not even a little bit of you that fancies a change?" Charlie pushed the box of dyes towards Tamara again, coaxing. "Aren't you a little bit tired of living by everyone else's rules?"

Deliberating quietly, Tamara eyed Charlie and then the hair

Chapter Fifteen

dye. "And you know what you're doing?"

"Absolutely." *Sort of.* Charlie had dyed her bandmates' hair plenty of times, and dyed the ends of her own in a rainbow of colours back before she'd chopped it all off.

"Fine." Snatching the hair dye box, Tamara marched back out of the kitchen. "Come on then. But I swear to God, if you make me look like a Smurf, we're getting a divorce."

* * *

Half an hour later, Charlie was hovered over Tamara in the bathroom, combing lilac dye through her blonde hair with plastic-gloved fingers. Tamara watched warily, keeping the towel tucked around her shoulders as her scalp began to stain purple. Still, anticipation bubbled in her. She needed a change. Needed to remind herself her body was her own, not anyone else's.

"How'd you get into modelling, then?" Charlie asked, playing the role of chatty hairdresser perfectly. Or, almost perfectly. Her eyes kept locking on Tamara's in the mirror. Ever since the kiss, tension sizzled constantly between them. They hadn't taken things further. Tamara refused to have sex with her on reality TV. She wanted to wait, and Charlie hadn't pushed. But that wasn't to say Tamara didn't sometimes regret her decision.

"It wasn't easy. Not many people wanted plus-size bodies when I was starting out, so I tried to gain a following on Instagram first. I found myself an agent, Nadine, and the jobs slowly started coming in."

"Did you always want to do it?"

Tamara shrugged. "I didn't think I could do it for a long time. Not unless I lost weight. But I was so sick of feeling bad about

First Comes Marriage

myself because people were afraid to show off fat bodies, and I was sick of feeling like I had to be insecure about mine. My auntie used to show me her old clothes catalogues." Her eyes turned glossy for her teenage self, still trying to find her place in the world. She still was sometimes, but then, her sense of worth had been centred around her body. Now, she knew there was far more to her. Her body was just one glorious aspect of many. "They were full of women with curves, and it was the first time I realised they even existed. I was only thirteen or fourteen. I ended up cutting out the pictures and making collages. Before that, though, I wanted to be a makeup artist. Not that I was any good."

"I suppose I never realised how rare it is to see a curvy girl on a poster or in a magazine." Charlie bit her lip, massaging the dye into Tamara's roots slowly. Her scalp tingled with her touch. "I've always been built like a pencil so it was never something I thought about."

Tamara snorted. "All my friends were too. I hated them for it."

"Well… now teenage girls get to see you when they open social media or a magazine. That's pretty bloody wonderful." Charlie's voice softened, her fingers stilling in Tamara's hair. "I'm sorry for the way I treated you when we met, Tam. For acting like you were just some superficial model. You're so much more than that."

A lump rose in Tamara's throat. She'd almost forgotten the way Charlie had brushed her off as unintelligent, fake, ditsy the day of their wedding. She hadn't expected an apology. That Charlie was able to give her one only proved she wasn't afraid of owning up to her mistakes, just as she had with the ones made before they'd met.

Chapter Fifteen

"Thank you," Tamara whispered.

Charlie's smile wobbled as she peeled off her gloves. "Well, I think we're done. It takes half an hour to develop, and I'm bloody starving. Breakfast?"

Tamara nodded, warily eyeing her reflection a final time before taking Charlie's hand.

Chapter Sixteen

Charlie had been wrong about the hot air balloon. After washing Tamara's dye from her hair with the showerhead, she'd found another note posted through the door. This one told her a car was waiting outside to take her to her challenge.

Why the hell hadn't she just left her answer as a fivesome? Why, why, why had she been honest when she knew it would leave her open and vulnerable to people who would use it against her? She knew the answer. Because she couldn't hide from Tamara.

Tamara appeared on the stairs after her hairdryer quietened, her new lilac curls bouncing as she skipped down. She shone with a wide grin, flicking her hair dramatically halfway down to show it off.

Thoughts of the note abandoned, Charlie couldn't help but marvel. The lilac brought out the pink in Tamara's cheeks and the blue in her eyes. She glowed with happiness, looking brand new. Angelic.

Chapter Sixteen

"You look…" Charlie stuttered over her own words as Tamara hopped off the bottom step. "You look really beautiful, Tam. How do you feel?"

"Good. I love it." Tamara's eyes shimmered with joy, and Charlie wanted her to always look this happy. It made her happy, too. Made her chest sing. It took her a moment to work out the lyrics: *my wife.*

She jolted with the realisation, dread slicing through her. What was she doing? They had seven weeks left of the experiment if they even made it that far, and then… then it was back to reality. She couldn't start thinking of Tamara as *hers*, because soon, it would all be over.

"Well… I think maybe we have plans," Charlie said in an attempt to push the thoughts away. Still, they lingered like a black cloud at the edge of her mind. She showed Tamara the letter, watching her features crumple with focus.

"Oh my God! Do you think—?"

"I'm in denial," Charlie said.

"But it's going to be so fun!" Tamara practically squealed, clapping and bouncing up and down on the spot. "A hot air balloon! I've always wanted to go on one!"

Before Charlie could grumble her own irrational fears aloud, her face was imprisoned by Tamara's hands, a soft peck placed on her nose. She smelled of the fruity conditioner Charlie had lathered into her hair not so long ago: berries and sharp chemicals.

"It's going to be fun," Tamara repeated, this time in a whisper.

Charlie wasn't sure yet if she believed it, so she clutched Tamara's hand and together they went outside.

* * *

First Comes Marriage

Charlie felt like an absolute arse. She'd be fine with putting her pride aside and admitting she was terrified were it not for the camera crew who had followed them here. "Here" being a farm a half-hour's drive away from the village. The rainbow-striped balloon sat in the middle of the field, waiting. Tamara hadn't let go of her hand yet, and Charlie was both grateful and irritated. She had a strong urge to run, much like the day of the wedding.

"Ready?" Tamara asked, squeezing her hand.

"No," Charlie replied bluntly. It didn't seem fair that Tamara was more excited about this. She'd gotten pretty hair and a fun hot air balloon ride out of today, and Charlie had only gotten anxiety.

Tipping her chin smugly, Tamara smirked, "Thought you were a rock star."

A challenge. One Charlie willingly accepted. She narrowed her eyes, steeling herself before dragging Tamara into the basket. The pilot introduced herself as Shannon and briefed them on all sorts of things that Charlie was too nervous to focus on. It was an effort not to stick her head out of the basket and vomit. She didn't feel sturdy even on the ground, let alone once they got into the air.

Tamara, on the other hand, seemed in her element, nodding along to Shannon's lecture like a pro. The cameras panned around Charlie, expecting some sort of reaction from her. She almost wanted to give them her middle finger. They were the same people who had put her on the show with Sloan. The same vultures who just wanted entertainment, no matter the cost.

Warmth caressed her back suddenly. Tamara had placed her hand on the base of Charlie's spine.

"Ready, then?" Shannon asked.

Chapter Sixteen

"No," Charlie said at the same time Tamara said, "Yes."

Shannon opened a valve overhead and they began to rise. Though the movement was slow, Charlie's stomach swooped and she clutched Tamara tighter, wrapping her arms around her waist. Tamara giggled, nestling her nose into Charlie's neck, "We're fine. I've got you."

But Charlie's eyes fell shut as they floated higher, nausea swimming in her gut. "I can't look." The wind whistled through her hair and stung her cheeks, cooler up here than below.

After what felt like an eternity, Tamara said softly, "Charlie, open your eyes."

Charlie trusted her. She could do nothing but trust her. So she opened her eyes, gripping the basket until her knuckles turned white. The world whooshed away beneath her feet, but she remained suspended — in the clouds. Fragments of blue peeked out of the white wisps, the sunlight fractured and golden as the afternoon idled on without them. There was nothing but sky and fields for miles. Endless. She'd never seen or felt anything like it.

She hadn't even realised her gasp until Tamara sidled closer, snaking an arm around Charlie's waist. "The cottages are over there." She pointed in the direction they'd come from, where a heart-shaped cluster of miniature lego-like buildings nestled into the countryside. The village was so small from up here. So meaningless.

Tamara's sniffle snagged Charlie's attention from the view. She was midway through wiping away a tear—not quickly enough. Her lavender hair floated behind her, eyes a brighter shade of blue so close to the sky.

"What's up?" Charlie asked, concern hardening her voice.

Tamara only shook her head, attempting to hide her face

First Comes Marriage

by burying herself into Charlie, her head resting against her shoulder. Charlie craned her neck to look at her, afraid now. A moment ago she'd been fine. Now she was crying. Charlie hadn't even said anything… had she? Maybe she was so used to talking unfiltered rubbish that she'd blurted something without noticing.

"Tam?" she begged. "Why are you crying, love?"

"They're happy tears," Tamara assured, voice thick as she drew the sleeves of her sweater over her hands and brought them to her mouth. She did that a lot at home, when she was tired or quiet, she'd trace the corner of her sleeve across her lips over and over. A comfort thing. It was endearing.

Home. Charlie realised too late that's what she thought of the cottage as. Their home.

"You should tell your face that," she quipped gently, parting from her to look at her properly. She tucked Tamara's hair away, cupping her round cheeks in her hands.

Tamara gave her a weak, watery smile. "I'm just going to hold onto this for a long time, that's all. I'll miss it. I'll miss all of this."

I'll miss you. Though it wasn't spoken, Charlie heard the words, and a sharp pang sliced through her. She forgot sometimes that this wasn't forever. That it was never meant to be this good or have come this far.

"Do you ever think the Cupids really got it right with us?" Tamara continued, tucking herself back into Charlie's shoulder to admire the view. "Like maybe we *are* compatible?"

Charlie had wondered. She'd wondered if the experts had known just how badly she needed someone like Tamara. Someone steady and accepting and warm. She wanted to tell her that. Wanted to tell Tamara she was everything Charlie

Chapter Sixteen

hadn't known she needed. But that wasn't compatibility, was it? It was just a coincidence. They hadn't put them together because they'd thought they would fall in love. They put them together because it would make good TV.

"Maybe," was all Charlie said, not quite believing it.

She noticed then that Shannon was watching them, expression filled with fondness. "You two are so cute. I've been watching you every night, you know. I'm actually a big fan of yours."

Charlie smiled politely, though dread always filled her when someone named themselves a fan. Worse because that someone was operating a basket that was currently defying the laws of gravity and could quite as easily send them careening to the ground. "Cheers."

"I knew it wasn't all an act," Shannon continued. "People keep saying it's all for the cameras, but... you can't fake what you two have. It's lovely."

"It's hard not to get used to somebody when you're stuck with them twenty-four hours a day," Charlie replied.

Slowly, Tamara tugged away, eyes narrowing for just a moment before she pasted on a smile. Charlie knew her well enough now to spot when it was forced, fake, and this smile was for Shannon's benefit. Charlie searched her, wondering what was wrong, but Tamara turned her back and continued her chat with Shannon. She barely looked at Charlie again for the rest of the ride, and Charlie was too stuck in her own head, in Tamara's words about compatibility, to dare ask why.

Chapter Seventeen

Tamara had been avoiding Charlie for the past week. She'd realised during the hot air balloon ride that Charlie didn't want the things Tamara wanted. She didn't feel the way Tamara felt. She was "stuck" with Tamara. That's what she'd told Shannon. It didn't matter that they'd kissed without cameras or spent their nights acting as though they knew one another inside out. It wasn't real. It would never be real for Charlie. Tamara was just a circumstance, not a choice.

It had been frosty in the cottage, but the main house wasn't much better as everyone piled into the sitting room the day before the vote-out. The result would be announced on live TV tomorrow night, and by the looks of it, they had one last challenge before the first couple departed.

"A lie detector test," Shell read from the card. That explained all the wires, machinery, and the man seated behind them at the table. "Now is your chance to ask your partner any burning questions. Viewers have also sent in their questions for you

Chapter Seventeen

to answer so they can decide who they wish to see stay in the village tomorrow evening."

"This is more drama than I signed up for," Charlie murmured. As she'd done all week, Tamara barely nodded. It was hard to so much as look at her without forgetting all sense of reason. Without forgetting that this was just a show, and everything had been fake. It had to have been.

Charlie was right, though. Jack and Gabby took the first round and it ended in tears when Gabby asked him if he fancied other women in the show. He pointedly looked at Shell before saying, "No." Which, of course, was labelled a lie by the examiner. The drama that ensued made Tamara and Charlie's relationship seem wonderful in comparison. Apparently, Shell and Jack had shared more than a bit of eye contact in the pantry the other day.

"Fucking hell, what a shitshow," Charlie murmured. She tried to grab Tamara's hand. Tamara didn't pull away, instead letting hers lie limply on her lamp while Charlie squeezed. "Glad I'm married to you."

Married to me or stuck with me? She bit her tongue. She'd vowed to herself that she wouldn't have this fight on the show. They'd talk about it when they left. When Charlie was no longer *stuck* with her.

Finally, Charlie's turn to get wired up came. She sat at the table, jaw clenched as Tamara was handed a pile of cue cards with the viewers' questions. She didn't want to explore any of her own. Not when she already knew the answer. So, she went straight to them.

"What did you think when you first saw me walking down the aisle?"

"You were gorgeous. Not my type, like, but I thought you

149

First Comes Marriage

were gorgeous. Course I did." Charlie licked her lips slowly, lines etched into her forehead.

"True," the man reading the data said.

Rafi let out an "*aw*" that Tamara tried to ignore, along with the blush warming her cheeks and the fluttering in her belly. She went to the next card.

"Do you have romantic feelings for me?"

"Yes." Charlie didn't even miss a beat. Again, it was supposedly true. Tamara wished she could believe it.

With a sigh, she paused on the next question, ice pooling through her veins. She already knew the answer to this one, yet still, she needed to hear it. To let go, she needed to hear it. "Do you see a future with us outside of the show?"

Charlie paused, swallowing thickly. Her eyes were pleading as though wishing Tamara could take it back. An answer in itself. She shifted and then was reprimanded by the examiner at the table. Apparently, too much movement might interfere with the results.

"Of course," she rasped finally.

Tamara didn't need the examiner to tell her it was a lie. There was no commitment in her voice. Only doubt. But he said it anyway: "Lie."

Everyone gasped.

"I'm not..." Charlie stumbled over her own words. "I just don't know, Tam, all right? We're so different. It would take a lot of work. But of course I want to try."

Working hard to keep her features smooth, emotionless, Tamara flicked to the final card. Her breath hitched in her throat at the words printed there: *Are you falling in love with me?*

She couldn't ask that. Not here, in front of everyone. She

150

Chapter Seventeen

couldn't face that type of rejection.

She put the cards face-down on the couch beside her. "That's it."

Charlie sighed in relief, pulling off the blood pressure cuff and the equipment clipped to her fingertip to measure perspiration. The examiner helped her with the wires attached to her stomach.

And then it was Tamara's turn. She took a deep breath and walked stiffly to the chair, the examiner setting up the equipment. She felt as though she were a criminal in an interrogation room. This entire thing was stupid. A reminder of why she was really here. Not for marriage. Not even a little bit.

"Fucking hell," Charlie announced as she read the first question. "Not asking that."

"Oh, come on!" Shell snatched the cards, eyes sparkling with mischief. "Have you ever cheated in a relationship?"

The rumours from her first marriage still hadn't worn off then. Tamara replied flatly, "No. Never."

"True," the examiner said.

With more force than expected, Charlie tugged the cards back. "Good job you didn't get that question, isn't it, Shell? It's my turn, so keep your beak out."

Tamara wanted to cringe, but she stayed still as possible.

Charlie stared at the next card for less than a moment before tossing it aside. "Fuck these. They're all so personal."

"Oh, come on. Everyone else had to!" Shell piped up bitterly. "That's not fair. If we have to air all our dirty laundry, so do you!"

"Just ask me anything. It doesn't matter." Tamara closed her eyes, at the end of her tether. She wanted to cry, and she wasn't

First Comes Marriage

even sure why.

"No. This is just stupid—"

"Just get it over with!" Tamara shouted desperately. For the first time since arriving here, she wanted to go home.

Silence fell like a heavy blanket across the sitting room. Charlie's eyes were dark, assessing. Finally, she said, "Fine. Why are you so mad at me?"

Tamara regretted asking her to continue. "I'm not mad at you."

"Lie," the examiner said.

She clamped her lips together, chest clenching tightly. Charlie raised her brows. "You *are* mad at me. Why?"

Tamara stayed quiet. She couldn't do this in front of everyone.

"You told me to ask, so I'm asking. Why are you mad at me?" Charlie repeated.

"Because you said you only like me because you're stuck with me." A breath puffed from Tamara at the end of the sentence, as though letting go of more than just the words. As though letting go of everything. Only the sadness still clung to her. It was still there.

Charlie frowned, seconds passing as she processed the information. "*What?* When?"

"Oh, fuck," Rafi muttered beside Alessandro.

Tears blurred Tamara's vision. She shook her head, tearing the equipment that bound her. She wouldn't do this. She hadn't come here to break her own heart, and certainly not for everyone to see. She'd made a mistake. The entire marriage had been a mistake. One she'd enjoyed far too much. One that hurt far too much.

She stood up and marched out of the sitting room, away from her audience, away from Charlie. As soon as she was out of

152

Chapter Seventeen

the main house, she tore off her microphone pack, dropping it in the grass. It was over. She had to leave. She couldn't stand another second of not knowing what was real.

"Tam!" Charlie breathlessly tried to catch up with her midway to the cottage. "What the fuck? What's going on?"

Tamara kept walking, muffling her sobs into her sleeves.

"Tamara!" Charlie was in front of her then, stopping her with her hands on Tamara's shoulders. "I don't understand why you're so upset. I didn't say I was only with you—"

"Yes, you did!" Tamara shouted. She'd had it constantly with Dominic. Being told that she was imagining every wrong thing he did, being told she was pathetic to get so upset. She wouldn't do it now. "You said it in the hot air balloon. I thought you really liked me for a minute, but you didn't. You're just stuck here. Stuck with me until we leave, and then we can go live out the futures you imagine, the ones where you've decided we aren't together."

"Are you serious?"

"Yes, I'm serious! I'm sick of being the person who's never chosen, Charlie. I'm *sick* of it. I came here…" She shook her head. She couldn't remember why she was here anymore. It was clear none of this was real. Maybe love wasn't real. Not for her. "It doesn't matter. I'm leaving."

"I don't know what you expected. *You* signed up for this." Charlie gritted her teeth, pulling Tamara back when she tried to leave. "You *wanted* me to be stuck with you. I played along with the plan, I got invested, I did the stupid tasks and dealt with Sloan. What more did you want from me?"

I wanted you to want me! Tamara wanted to scream. But she stifled it all down, unwilling to let her heart spill all over the grass. All over Charlie's shoes. It was quite clear Charlie didn't

153

First Comes Marriage

want it. She was just playing along, like she'd promised from the beginning. It was Tamara who had broken their agreement. Tamara who had ruined it with her feelings.

"Nothing," she said instead, voice sounding hollow to her own ears. "I want nothing from you, Charlie. Nothing at all."

And then she veered away from the cottage altogether, towards Cupid's Conservatory — to tell the producers she was done.

* * *

Charlie waited for Tamara to come back. She sat in the empty cottage for over an hour, expecting the door to open any moment. She didn't even know where Tamara could have gone, and nobody would tell her a thing. When someone finally let themselves in and filled her corridor, though, it wasn't Tamara. It was another producer. "Tamara has left the show," he said. "I'm sorry, Charlie. She's already on her way back to London."

For once, Charlie didn't have any smart retort or impulsive reaction. She stood, feeling empty, staring at the mug of cold tea on the coffee table. The one Tamara didn't have time to finish this morning. Charlie always knew it would end. It was why she hadn't allowed herself to think past the experiment. She didn't want to think about a future where Tamara would no longer be a permanent fixture in her daily life.

But that time was now. Tamara had made her own mind up. She hadn't wanted to talk or listen or fix things. Or stay. Charlie had done her best. She'd given Tamara more than she'd ever been willing to offer anyone before. She'd....

God, she'd felt things she didn't know were possible. She'd found a home. But it was gone now. It was all gone.

Chapter Seventeen

"Would you mind chatting to Sandra about what happened?" the producer asked.

Charlie set her chin, blinking back the numbness. It only made room for a heavy ache in her chest. "I don't have anything to say. I want to go home, too."

Home. Where the fuck was home? She didn't have one. The cottage had become home. Tamara had become home. All she had was a hotel room and Jed, who would no doubt have plenty to say about this. Not that she gave a shit. It wasn't about her career anymore. Her reputation. It hadn't been for a while.

The producer nodded, surprisingly sympathetic. "Okay. I'll arrange that now. You can pack your things if you like. If you change your mind…."

But Tamara hadn't changed hers, and Charlie was too stubborn to do the same. So, she packed her things and left the same way Tamara had: without a word.

Chapter Eighteen

"What the fuck happened?" were the first words out of Jed's mouth the following day, when he barged into Charlie's hotel room, the same one she'd stayed in the night before moving into the village. She'd felt barely anything then. Only that same anger that plagued her always, made worse when she was about to subject herself to at least two months of hell.

But it hadn't been hell. It had been the opposite.

She swallowed the lump in her throat, the one that had been lodged there since she'd gotten into the car and rolled away from the cottage. It was the first time in six weeks she'd been without Tamara, and it was too quiet, too stifling.

"Don't," she warned Jed, sinking onto the end of her bed and squeezing her eyes closed. Instinct had her fidgeting with the band on her finger. She hadn't been able to take it off yet. "Just don't. It wasn't my choice to leave."

Jed stopped in front of her, confusion muddying his eyes. "What happened?" he asked, softer now. Somehow, that was

Chapter Eighteen

worse. It meant he saw right through Charlie. Saw all the pain. For once, she was no good at hiding it. Didn't even have the energy to try.

"I don't know," she admitted. "Tamara left." *She left me.*

"Did you have a fight?" He sat on the bed beside her, his knees brushing hers. "You were doing so well, you and her. I was... well, I was surprised at how well you two were getting on. You seemed to really like each other. Even the public was backing you. What went wrong?"

She realised then it wouldn't have aired yet. The lie detector. The fight outside, which hopefully wouldn't be shown. Some of their most important moments had been behind closed doors. Their first kiss. Their last. It hadn't all been fake. Far from it.

"I don't know what happened," she repeated, hands curling into fists. "One minute, we were okay. And then she just blew up because apparently I said something she didn't like. She didn't even talk to me. She just... she just left. Do you know where she is?" She'd already asked at reception, but the answer had been no. She didn't even have Tamara's number. Married, with no way of contacting her wife.

Jed shook his head solemnly. "Nadine was waiting here for her yesterday, but she said someone called and asked her to meet Tamara at her house in Notting Hill. She didn't want to come back to the hotel or talk to anyone from the show."

Of course that's where she lived. Jesus Christ. Despite the knot beneath her ribs, warmth filtered through Charlie and she almost laughed. Instead, she pinched the bridge of her nose. "Fuck."

He raised his brows. "You really like her, don't you?"

"I..." Charlie opened her mouth to reply, but it was lost in her throat. Because the answer should have been no. She shouldn't

First Comes Marriage

have liked Tamara. She'd meant what she'd said during the lie detector test. She had no idea how this could work in the outside world. They were so different. Tamara was classy and kind and Charlie was… a mess.

And yet the answer wasn't no. Not by a long shot.

"Thought so." Jed smirked, nudging her knowingly. "She's good for you, you know. I thought you'd been given tranquilisers when I saw you in there. Walking away from Sloan the way you did. Keeping your cool when people pushed your buttons. It was her, though, wasn't it? She brought out the best in you. You almost seemed happy."

"Not happy enough, apparently."

"If you want to fix it, I have Nadine's number. I can find her address."

"There's nothing to fix. It's over," Charlie muttered, though she didn't quite believe it. Waking up in an empty bed that morning had left Charlie filled with a black silence. She'd even gone to make two cups of tea, only realising when the water had been poured.

Jed sighed and pulled out his phone. Charlie almost protested, icy fear running through her at the thought of him asking for Tamara's address anyway. But he didn't, instead opening Twitter and clicking on the official *First Comes Marriage UK* account. He scrolled down through endless tweets, some of them including Charlie and Tamara — with *#Tamarlie* at the end of each post, which made her roll her eyes. Finally, he stopped on a video and handed the phone over.

"You should watch this."

Tamara's face, glowing beneath studio lighting, filled the screen. It was her opening tape, filmed before the experiment began, with Sandra asking the questions. Charlie hadn't taken

158

Chapter Eighteen

her interview seriously, finding it too much like therapy, but as she pressed play, she realised Tamara... well, Tamara had.

"*What would your ideal relationship look like?*" Sandra asked, seated opposite Tamara in an armchair with a pink, heart-shaped back.

Tamara smiled in the video, wistful and mesmerising. Charlie's wife. Her stomach clenched with longing. "*Well... if my first marriage taught me anything, it's that you can't expect 'ideal.' It shouldn't be about what you want from someone or what you can take. All I really want is for someone to look at me and not want to change me. To accept me and love me as I am, even if what I am isn't their ideal. I want someone to* choose *me, not just settle for me until something better comes along.*"

Sandra tilted her head. "*Have you ever had that before? Have you ever been accepted and loved as you are?*"

Tamara's chin wobbled, and a crack began splitting through Charlie's heart. "*No. I don't feel like I have.*"

"*You've never felt chosen?*" Sandra probed in that awful, persistent way that either forced you to clam up and put up your guards or the opposite. Charlie had done the former, but she could see Tamara's pain, her emotions, spilling out of that chair with the tears.

"*No. Not without conditions,*" Tamara answered, voice quivering. "*People choose certain parts of me, and when I'm not what they hoped for, they give up.*"

"*What is marriage to you?*"

"*A promise. A partnership.*" Tamara dabbed her eyes with a tissue. "*Something that goes beyond a bit of paper. Something that you choose not just on your wedding day, but every day after.*"

And Charlie had implied that she was stuck with Tamara. That she hadn't chosen her. No wonder she'd stewed on it

First Comes Marriage

for so long. No wonder she was so upset. Their relationship had blurred the lines. It had become real. But Charlie had still been wrapped up in the "showmance" of it all, certain that Tamara would continue her glamorous life in one direction while Charlie drank and partied in the opposite one. She only realised now it wasn't what she wanted. She wanted what she'd had in the cottage. She wanted comfort and laughter and someone to have her back. Not just anyone.

She wanted Tamara.

"I've made a mistake, Jed," Charlie said.

"I think that's the first time I've ever heard you say that," Jed replied, closing the video. "Shall I get the address?"

She could no longer see another option.

Chapter Nineteen

Tamara could admit she'd missed her home: the smell of her Madagascan vanilla candles, the warm, cashmere throw she was currently huddled up in, her ugliest, fluffiest pyjamas she'd been advised by Nadine to leave at home.

Still, it was an odd feeling to be sitting on her own couch, Nadine watching her intently from the armchair opposite. A hole had opened up inside her, and she wasn't sure how to fill it. She wasn't sure what to do at all. She just wanted to mope.

"I really think you should talk to her," Nadine said, sipping her steaming coffee from a rainbow-patterned mug. "I think maybe you jumped to conclusions too quickly."

"No." Tamara played with the string of her teabag, watching it bob up and down in her mug. "She was pretty clear. This was never permanent for her."

"It's been six weeks, Tammy. Maybe she's still figuring it out. It wasn't supposed to be permanent for either of you until you got in there. It must be confusing, trying to figure out what's real."

First Comes Marriage

"Well, I don't want her to be confused. I don't want to be pushed aside again. I don't want her to be stuck with me." Tamara bit her wobbling lower lip. "I'm sure I seem like a complete drama queen. But my marriage with Dominic... realising he didn't love me... it nearly broke me. I can't do it again. I deserve better than to have to question whether I'm truly wanted."

"You really liked her that much?" Nadine didn't bother to hide her surprise. "Charlie Dean?"

Tamara rested her head against the back of her velvety couch, trying not to cry again. It was no easy feat. "She's different when you get to know her. The arrogant rock star thing is just a mask."

"*Hmm.*" Nadine lay back in the chair, curling her feet up beneath her and turning on the wall-mounted television. "Fancy a film?"

"Anything." Tamara couldn't pretend to care. She went back to staring at her tea as Nadine picked something to watch, not noticing she'd opened YouTube until Charlie's voice echoed around the living room. She whipped her head up, seeing the caption: *First Comes Marriage Day 14: Charlie Dean in Cupid's Conservatory.*

Charlie sat on the loveseat in the conservatory they'd all had to venture to several times a week to talk to Sandra. Her arms were crossed, expression as impatient as ever as Sandra questioned her: *"How are things with Tamara?"*

"They're... surprisingly good." Charlie began smoothing down the rose-patterned pillows.

"Why 'surprisingly'?" Sandra asked.

A shrug. *"I just didn't expect her to be... well, her. Or I guess I didn't expect to like her so much."*

Chapter Nineteen

"What is it about Tamara you like?"

More fidgeting as Charlie deliberated, twisting the red fringe of the cushions around her fingers now. *"Everything, really. She's funny. She listens when people speak. She understands. She always smells nice, and she never gets annoyed with me when I'm grumpy. She laughs like... I don't know. Like it's the last time she'll ever get the chance. She puts all of herself into everything, you know? And she always asks me how I slept in the morning, like we haven't been lying next to each other all night. But it's not just a throwaway thing. She wants to know the answer."*

Sandra's lips spread slowly with a proud smile as she crossed one leg over the other. *"It sounds like perhaps you might be falling in love."*

Charlie scoffed. Of course she did.

"Have you ever had a relationship like this before?" coaxed Sandra.

"An arranged marriage aired on national telly? No, can't say I have."

Sandra clasped her hands patiently. *"I mean what you just described. Waking up beside someone who cares about how you slept. Having someone listen to you and understand. Have you had a partner who does that for you before?"*

"I haven't had a partner who sticks around for more than a night, so we could start there."

"Was that your choice or theirs?"

"Both. I wasn't exactly seeking out long-term," Charlie said.

"Interesting." Sandra focused on Charlie with her piercing stare. *"Then this is new for you."*

"Very new."

"Do you miss your old lifestyle?"

Charlie leaned back, tilting her head to the glass ceiling for

163

First Comes Marriage

only a moment before she said, *"No. Not particularly. I'd rather be here, I think."*

"And what about when you leave the experiment? Would you want to keep Tamara in your life?"

Her knee began to bounce nervously, and she played with the wedding band on her finger. *"Things would definitely feel a bit emptier without her now."*

The video ended, and Nadine turned it off, casting Tamara a pointed look. Tamara didn't know what to do or say. She'd assumed Charlie would have been difficult, evasive, in those sessions with Sandra, just like she had been at the wedding. She hadn't known....

Nobody had ever talked about her that way. As though she were an important — *vital* — part of their life.

She didn't even realise her cheeks were damp until a tear rolled down her neck. She swiped her face with the sleeve of her cardigan quickly. *It doesn't matter*, she told herself. What Charlie said about their future was right. They'd never work. No matter what Charlie had told Sandra, she'd still made her mind up in the weeks that followed.

"If that clip is anything to go off, I think you were pretty wanted, Tammy," Nadine said quietly. "I watched you with her every night. You were... electric. That kiss in the kitchen. The way she chased after you. The way you talked about each other in the conservatory. God, you even dyed your hair for her. We watched her fall in love with you. Whether she wants to admit it or not, she cares. She has to. She couldn't fake what we just saw. I can't believe I'm talking about Charlie Dean when I say all this, but... I think it would be worth talking to her. She might surprise you."

"I need time. I...." Tamara took a shuddering breath, aching

Chapter Nineteen

all over. She wanted so badly to believe Nadine was right, but she wasn't sure anymore. "Would you mind giving me a bit of time to think?"

"Of course." Nadine smiled sadly and abandoned her coffee on the table, shrugging on her coat. "I'm here if you need me."

"Thank you."

She squeezed Tamara's shoulder, and then was gone. The sound of the door falling shut felt as loud as an explosion in the sudden emptiness. Tamara sat, staring into space, wondering what the hell came next. It was the first time she'd been alone in six weeks, and it didn't provide the comfort she'd hoped for. It only made her lonelier.

A knock on the door drew her out of her reverie. She huffed, standing up and going to the door. Probably the postman, he was there constantly with sponsored products gifted from different brands. But when Tamara opened the door, it wasn't parcels that were waiting for her. It was Charlie.

Wearing glasses Tamara had never seen before. She hadn't even had contact lenses in the cottage.

Tamara's heart stopped completely, though the world outside kept spinning. Cars passed down her avenue. The neighbours mowed their lawn. Charlie kept looking at her through those strange, old-fashioned lenses.

"You live in Notting Hill. I live on a tour bus. Everyone in the world knows who we are," Charlie began after clearing her throat. "But… I'm also just a girl, standing in front of a girl, asking her to love her." She frowned. "Wait, that's too many 'her' pronouns in one sentence, isn't it? It's like they didn't even think about the lesbians when they wrote this quote. Let me—"

"Charlie… what the hell are you doing?" Tamara interrupted, bundling her blanket closer as though it might protect her from

165

First Comes Marriage

the hurt.

"I'm being a mash-up of Hugh Grant and Julia Roberts, 'cause I know you fancy them both. It's a grand gesture."

"How did you even find out where I lived?"

"Jed asked Nadine." Charlie smiled wryly and then, against Tamara's blank stare, huffed and ripped off her glasses. "Look, I didn't realise the weight of what I said about you and me when I said it. I was never *stuck* with you, alright? If I wanted to leave, I would have. But I didn't. Because...." She licked her lips as though the words burned before they could leave her mouth.

"Because?" Tamara raised her eyebrow, clutching the door-jamb to keep her upright when dizziness began to tingle through her.

"Because it was real for me," Charlie said quietly. "Being with you was the most real thing I've ever had, and I didn't want to think about what came next. I didn't expect you to want to think about it either. I'm not good like you are, Tamara. I make an idiot of myself and I do the wrong thing and I've hurt a lot of people by being reckless and arrogant. I didn't want you to end up being one of those people. But then I realised that you wouldn't be. You wouldn't be, because you're my wife and I'm falling in love with you, and I *choose* you. I choose us. And I want to fight to keep it. No more fucking up and letting you go. I want this. I want you."

Tears streamed down Tamara's face. She stifled a sob as everything she'd ever dreamed of feeling washed over her. "You really mean that?"

"Do you think I'd be here looking like a nob if I didn't?" Charlie asked bluntly, waving the glasses around. "I'm sorry, Tam. Please... *Please* be my wife again."

Tamara had never stopped. She still wore the ring. Unable

Chapter Nineteen

to stop herself with doubts and fears, she pulled Charlie into a tight hug. A chuckle vibrated from Charlie, and then she was pulling away, kissing away Tamara's tears. "Can't believe you live in Notting Hill, you big sap."

Tracing Charlie's sharp jaw, Tamara laughed, "Coming from the woman who just quoted the film."

"Yeah, well…" Charlie pecked Tamara's nose softly, gazing at her intently, "anything for you, love."

Finally, Tamara saw it was true. Charlie Dean would give her anything she asked for and Tamara would offer the same for the woman she loved. The woman who had been chosen for her, but also the woman she'd chosen for herself.

Perhaps the Cupids had known what they were doing after all.

Epilogue

Tamara watched proudly from backstage as Charlie performed to her crowd, her voice raspy and mellow as she played her newest single, which had gone to number one last weekend. Since marrying her very own rock star a year ago, Tamara's life had changed in all sorts of ways. They had a golden retriever waiting for them at their Notting Hill home, for starters, and her nights were balanced between watching Charlie's gigs, going to fancy parties with friends, or falling asleep at nine p.m. with one of Tamara's rom-coms still playing on the telly. While Charlie worked all day in the studio, Tamara booked more shoots than ever and had even become the creative consultant of Halliday, a high-end plus-size clothing brand brought to life by one of the most talented designers in the world, Francesca Halliday. Her life was a dream. One she never wanted to wake up from.

"Boo," a voice whispered in her ear. She turned to find Jed and tugged him into a hug excitedly. Behind him, four familiar faces waited: the members of Ghost Song. It had been a long road

Epilogue

for Charlie to regain their friendship, particularly Yasmin's, but she was trying, and everyone could see it. There had been no more broken guitars or cameras since they'd left the cottage, and no more Sloans either. Charlie was ready to move on from her mistakes, and Tamara had held her hand throughout every moment of it.

As she greeted each of them in turn, she heard the crowd scream behind the curtain. Charlie's voice boomed through the microphone, breathless. "This next one is a special one for my gorgeous wife, Tamara." Another roar of cheers left Tamara wanting to shrink. She'd had no idea Charlie would be singing something for her tonight. "Funnily enough, it was the song she walked down the aisle to. Sing along if you know the words."

A slowed-down version of "Will You Still Love Me Tomorrow" was strummed from Charlie's acoustic guitar, and then she began to sing, more softly and stripped back than Tamara had ever heard. Tears filled her eyes as she remembered the wedding. She hadn't known then that Charlie really was the right person for her, but she did now. Even when she woke up grumpy or complained about seeing Hugh Grant on telly again.

She was Tamara's wife, and she chose Charlie every day. She would keep choosing her. She'd made a vow, after all.

About the Author

Bryony Rosehurst is a British romance author dedicated to telling diverse stories of love and happily ever afters — and perhaps a little bit of angst sprinkled in for good measure. You can usually find her painting (badly), photographing new cities (occasionally), or wishing for autumn (always). Chat with her on Twitter: @BryonyRosehurst.

Also by Bryony Rosehurst

while the rest of the world dances: poems
while the rest of the world dances is a collection of poems surrounding personal experiences of mental and chronic illness, relationships, coming of age, inequality, and other life experiences, both good and bad, with the parts separated into seasons.

her roots were planted in cold, black mud,
 not enough water,
 not enough love,
 not enough sunlight,
 so she forgot to grow.

don't put her leaves in your mouth:
 this soil has always been poison,
 and now she is, too.

Love, Anon: a festive fake dating novella (Hayes Family, #1
Christmas is approaching and Arden Hayes is in dire need of a date if only to convince her concerned family that she's moved on from her failed marriage.

Rosie Gladwell is lonely in a city that isn't hers, an ocean away from home, and every date that she's been on ends in disaster. When she comes across an advertisement for someone willing to act as a Christmas date on new social media and dating app, Don't Be a Stranger, she responds in the hopes that she won't have to spend Christmas alone — even if it means spending the night pretending to be in a relationship with a stranger. However, as Rosie and Arden get to know one another, they seem to find an instant, undeniable connection. Is it as real as it feels, or just another act?

Meet Me on St. Patrick's Day: A contemporary romance novel (Hayes Family, #2)
Is it just the (bad) luck of the Irish that keeps pushing Brennan and Quinn together, or something more?

Quinn Hayes and Brennan O'Keeffe are nothing more than perfect strangers, but when their paths cross often over the years, always on St. Patrick's Day, they realise that they seem to share a connection they've never been able to find with anyone else. Their personal lives are messy and chaotic and ever-changing in so many ways, but their link always remains the same — until a struggling, troubled Quinn makes a misguided mistake, and as a result, believes she has lost Brennan for good.

Years later, she unknowingly walks into his bar, and their lives become entangled once again, with Quinn landing a bar tending job as Brennan's co-worker at Irish pub, O'Keeffe's. Will they finally get it right this time, or will Brennan's secrets and Quinn's shadowy past ruin everything once and for all?

On Common Ground: a second chance romance novella (Hayes Family, #3)
World famous fashion designer Francesca Halliday always has somewhere to be, but when her private jet is forced to make an emergency landing due to an unexpected storm, she becomes stranded in the middle of the Scottish Highlands with the pilot, who is none other than Tristan Hayes, an old flame she never planned to see again.

Tristan is fresh out of his divorce and rattled by the reappearance of his ex-ex-ex-girlfriend, especially considering that he never got closure from their sudden break-up nine years ago. Stuck in the middle of nowhere in a terrible storm, will he finally understand the reason why Francesca left him behind to pursue her career, or will facing old wounds only put them more at odds with each other?

Cursed in Love: a WLW adventure romance novella

Ophelia is cursed. Ever since finding an old relic known as Eilidh's ring in the Scottish Highlands three years ago, rumoured to have belonged to a woman once scorned by an unfaithful lover, her love life has been on a downward spiral. When the opportunity comes to return the ring back to its resting place with its namesake, Ophelia seizes it with both hands in the hopes the curse will be lifted. However, when nervy, short-tempered, workaholic Luce is accidentally dragged into her antics (as well as down a couple of waterfalls) during Ophelia's attempt to commandeer her canoe, lifting the curse proves more difficult than planned — particularly with two con men trailing them in the hopes of getting their hands on a precious rare stone embedded within the relic.

With no way of getting Luce back to the campsite she'd been unwillingly holidaying in, where both her anxiety medication and comfort zone reside, she and Ophelia find themselves reluctant allies in their separate attempts to find peace. But hiking through the Hebrides in the middle of winter causes plenty of problems, and with the thieves closing in on Ophelia, tensions run high and feelings begin to develop. Will Luce and Ophelia find common ground and reveal themselves to one another as they work to get the ring back to the lake in which it was found, or will Ophelia be bound to the same tragic fate as Eilidh for the rest of her life?

Printed in Great Britain
by Amazon